SAVED BY TIME

BOOK NINE OF THE THISTLE & HIVE SERIES

JENNAE VALE

JENNAE VALE

Copyright © 2018 by Jennae Vale

All rights reserved.

No part of this book may be reproduced in any form or by any electronic or mechanical means, including information storage and retrieval systems, without written permission from the author, except for the use of brief quotations in a book review.

This book is a work of fiction. Names, characters, places, and incidents are products of the author's imagination or are used fictitiously. Any resemblance to actual events, locales, or persons, living or dead, is entirely coincidental.

❦ Created with Vellum

CHAPTER 1

The Thistle & Hive Inn - Scotland, Present Day

So, this is where the magic happens. Tina Carrera smiled to herself as she surveyed the lobby of The Thistle & Hive Inn. Her sister, Elle and her brother-in-law, Hamish were having a very animated conversation with Edna Campbell, the innkeeper witch who'd matched them. All Tina could think was how crazy it was that both Hamish and Elle had time traveled. And this adorable lady with the wild blue stripe in her white hair had made it happen. Crazy!

"I'm so happy to finally meet you," Elle said, speaking to Edna. "If it wasn't for you I would never have met Hamish and my career would have died an untimely death."

"Oh, 'twas nothing, dear. I do what I can when I see someone who needs a little love in their life." Edna grasped Hamish's hand. "What do ye think of modern-day Scotland, lad?"

"It's been five hundred years since I was last here," he chuckled and they all joined him. "'Tis different than I expected. We were in Edinburgh yesterday. 'Tis a big city."

"Did ye tour the castle?" she asked.

"Aye. A place I'd never had the pleasure to visit when I was with the Mackenzies."

"And who's this?" Edna asked.

"Tina, come over here," Elle called. "This is my sister, Tina. She's my tour manager."

"Oh. 'Tis a big job, aye?"

"I guess you could say that. Keeping these two under control is a bigger job," she teased. "I'm pleased to meet you, Edna." Tina had enjoyed being Elle's tour manager, but it certainly wasn't what she'd dreamed of doing. She was glad the tour was over and that for the foreseeable future there wouldn't be another one. It had been an experience she'd never forget, but she understood now that along with the thrill, it was also exhausting. It had been Elle's dream, not hers, but it had given her a bit more understanding into her sister's life. Tina wanted nothing more than to go back home and find her place in this world. She'd always wanted to be her own boss so following the schedule and demands of the touring company had been a big adjustment. She wasn't sure what she wanted to do, but she was certain that whatever it was would keep her a little closer to Carrera Ranch.

Edna continued chatting with Elle as she occasionally snuck a peek in Tina's direction. "How many more cities are ye going to before ye head home?"

"We're done. We made Edinburgh our final stop because we wanted to come see you, but after this we're heading home."

"I'm so pleased yer here. How long can ye stay?"

"It's going to be a quick visit. I'm exhausted," Elle said.

"Tell her," Hamish said, poking Elle in the side.

"Tell me what?" questioned Edna.

"Well, we wanted you to be one of the first to know. Tina's the only other person we've told."

"Aye," Edna said, patience obviously wearing thin.

"I'm pregnant!"

Edna's hands flew to her face as her eyes and mouth opened wide. "Oh! That's wonderful news!" Edna came around the desk to pull them both into a hug. She was beaming with obvious pride. "I knew ye'd be the perfect match. I cannae tell ye how happy I am for ye. How far along are ye?"

"Just about two months, but it's been difficult traveling. I've had morning sickness from the start," Elle said, rubbing her tummy.

"More like all day sickness," Tina added. Being pregnant wasn't high on her list after watching Elle barfing on a daily basis and getting nauseous at the drop of a hat. That did not look appealing to her at all.

"Ye poor dear. We will take good care of ye while yer here. Yer room is the first one at the top of the stairs. Why dinnae ye head on up to rest before dinner. Dylan, my nephew-in-law, is an amazing cook. Hopefully, ye'll be well enough to eat something."

"I hope so," Elle said, yawning.

"Come love," Hamish took her hand and headed for the stairs. "We'll be down for dinner."

"Good. I can't wait to hear all about ye two lovebirds." Edna turned her attention to Tina. "Tina, yer room will be right next to theirs, if ye'd like to head up."

"No. I think I'll stay down here if you don't mind." Tina could swear there was a new glint in Edna's eye, but it disappeared so fast she couldn't be sure.

"Of course I don't. Would ye care for something to drink. Tea?" Edna asked.

"Is that a bar I see?" Tina walked into the dining room and straight to the bar. "Where's the bartender?" she asked glancing around the room.

"Oh, we dinnae have one. Angus, my husband, makes drinks whenever someone would like one."

"I'd love a glass of wine, if that would be okay."

"Let me get us both a glass. Why dinnae ye sit over there by the window. We can get to know each other a wee bit better."

"I'd like that." Tina picked a table by the window, enjoying the sunshine peeking through and the fact that she could see what was happening here in Glendaloch. The tour had visited twenty cities in Europe. Tina had more stamps in her passport than she had ever dreamed, but it was all a blur. Airports, trains, a tour bus, hotels, venues, more hotels, dealing with logistics, constantly checking details for the next event and the one after that to make sure everything went smoothly for everyone else. There hadn't been any time for exploring the cities she had visited. She hadn't even had a chance to just sit and enjoy a quiet moment in months.

Being on tour was great in a lot of ways. She had spent months touring with her brothers and sister. They'd had a chance to work together and heal over some the hurt that had been a real wedge between them for years. She loved her family, loved being with them, but it was exhausting.

Edna joined her carrying two glasses of wine. "I hope ye like a nice sauvignon blanc. This one is quite good."

"It's almost as if you know me, Edna," Tina laughed. "How long have you lived in Glendaloch?"

"My whole life. I was born here."

"It's exactly what I thought a small Scottish village would look like. Very quaint." She took a sip of her wine, savoring the flavor. "Mmmm. This *is* good." Tina sighed, feeling some of the tension she had carried start to drain from her shoulders.

"I'm glad ye like it. Dylan and Maggie, my niece, go over to France occasionally and bring back some wonderful bottles. Ye'll have a chance to meet them later." Edna's smile was pleasant, friendly. There was something about her that made Tina want to confide in her. Ever since Elle had told her about traveling to the past, Tina had wondered about the woman, the witch, that had sent her there.

"So, Elle tells me you're a witch. Is that something you've always been, or did you have to learn how to be one?" Tina couldn't believe she had just blurted that out. She had meant to sort of ease into the topic.

Edna didn't seem surprised or offended, she just smiled and that glint from before made another appearance. "I've been a witch for as long as I can remember. No classes for me. It comes quite naturally."

"Interesting," Tina mused.

"What of ye? What do ye like to do when yer not on tour with yer sister."

"I live at home with my parents and some other family members. We have a ranch about an hour out of San Francisco. Elle and Hamish built a house next door to the family ranch, so we see them all the time."

"Isn't that lovely? It's so nice that yer family is a close one."

"We definitely are that." Tina took another sip of wine and thought about the tour bus, the tiny dressing rooms, "Sometimes a little too close."

"What do ye mean?"

"Family nosiness. Especially for me. Before the tour I had a job I didn't really like, spent a lot of time babysitting my niece and nephew. I didn't really go out or date." She shook her head. It wasn't that she didn't want to, it was more that the men she met inevitably had an agenda. Once they found out who her sister was, that was all she was to them – Elle's sister. "My mother can't understand why I'm not married and having children. She'll be so excited when she finds out about Elle."

"So yer mother is nosy?"

Tina started. That made her sound harsh. "I shouldn't have said it that way. I live with them, so they know all my business. They just want me to be happy."

"You're not?"

Tina shrugged her shoulders. "Happiness is different things to different people."

"What is it to ye?" Edna's cocked eyebrow and slightly tipped head showed her interest.

Tina thought back on the last few years, "I guess I don't have a good answer to that question," Tina admitted.

"Ye say yer Mum wants ye to be married. Do ye have a lad yer sweet on?"

Tina had to laugh at that. She loved Edna's accent. It was darling. "Nope. No one."

"Do ye wish ye did?"

"Sure. It's not that easy though. I've been traveling a lot and prior to that I'd had to resort to online dating, which is great for some people, but my experience has been that for men it's like they're kids in a candy shop. Oh, look at that girl and that one. They are never happy. Always looking for the next best thing… like that exists."

"That does sound terrible." Edna shook her head, Tina felt the pity Edna had for her and couldn't even bristle at it. She *was* pitiful. She needed change, needed something else in her life besides being in Elle's shadow.

"It is. I'm just tired of it all. I'd like to have someone I could spend time with. Someone I could depend on to be there for me, but it's looking less and less likely that it will happen." Tina was just plain tired of the whole mess. What was the point of trying? Nothing she did seemed to make a difference.

"'Tis a shame. Yer a lovely lass."

"Apparently not lovely enough," she chuckled, even though it was, in reality, a painful truth she lived with every day. She'd decided there had to be something wrong with her, although she couldn't pinpoint it. She did have a sharp tongue, but that shouldn't be a deal breaker. Anyone who knew her was aware that she was all bark and no bite.

"Well, I'm sure someone will come along soon. Yer too good to let get away." Edna sipped her wine, eyeing Tina over the rim of her glass.

"That's very sweet of you to say." Tina said. Edna was just being a good hostess, why else would she say that. She certainly didn't know her or know anything about her. She thought to change the subject. "So, tell me about this time travel you do."

"'Tis something I discovered many years ago. 'Tis how I met my husband Angus."

"Really?" Tina was impressed. She wondered how many others she'd helped find their love.

"Aye. He's a Highlander from Hamish's time. I must admit, I'm a bit of a busy body when it comes to helping others find the love of their life. So far I've done verra well at it. Perhaps I could help ye."

Was she reading Tina's thoughts?

Edna was eyeing her from head to toe with what appeared to be great curiosity. "Would ye like to give it a try?"

"Oh, I don't think so. I don't even like to fly. I've had a hard enough time traveling through Europe on this tour. Time travel might be pushing it too far." But her curiosity got the better of her. "Just out of curiosity, how would that work?"

"I'd send ye back in time to meet the one for ye. He's there and he's waiting for ye, though he doesnae ken it yet." Edna wore what Tina could only describe as a mischievous smile.

Butterflies had suddenly appeared in her stomach as she absorbed what Edna said. *He's waiting for ye.* That can't possibly be right, though. This was ridiculous. "I couldn't possibly do that. I've got to get back home." No. There was no way she was going to get talked into it.

"Whatever for? Ye've said there's no one there for ye, except yer family. Don't get me wrong, 'tis important, as Elle would tell ye now that she understands it."

"Yeah, she's a different person. She's all about the family now. From dinners together to traveling together, she's all about togetherness. Thank you for that." Tina really meant it. Having her sister back and completely present with the whole family was a gift she never expected. "Hamish has been a blessing to all of us. He has become a big part of our family and we all love him to pieces."

"I'm glad it all worked out." Edna was looking at her again with that odd expression that said she was peering into her soul. "Stay. Let me help ye."

"I'll think about it, but time travel seems scary to me. I have so many questions about how it works. What if I got stuck there? I couldn't take that chance." That settled it. She hoped that would put an end to this uncomfortable topic.

Edna laughed at her, "I can tell ye, I have never had anyone get stuck that didn't want to be." Tina wondered what on earth that meant. "I've got some important matters to attend to, but let's talk again later tonight or perhaps tomorrow. I'm sure I can convince ye."

Tina admired Edna's stick-to-itiveness. Persistence was a quality Tina was very familiar with as she possessed it herself. Once she made up her mind to do something, there was no one who could talk her out of it. No matter the obstacles, it was as good as done. "We'll see about that."

Edna winked at her as she left the room. She was met by an older gentleman who reminded Tina of Hamish. She guessed it must be Angus. A moment later when he took Edna in his arms and kissed her soundly on the lips, she was sure of it. She was not a voyeur, but she couldn't seem to take her eyes off of them. She could feel the love there, just as she could feel it from Elle and Hamish. It just didn't seem fair that every guy she ever dated was either completely not her type, or was only interested for a short time until that other girl came along. Why hadn't she found her special someone? Maybe she *should* give Edna a chance to do a little matchmaking for her.

～

They all ate dinner together in the dining room. It reminded her of dinners at the Carrera ranch back in California. Happy conversation, a good bit of teasing and delicious food. This time the chef wasn't her mother though. It was Dylan Sinclair from San Francisco. He was married to Edna's niece, Maggie. They were a cute couple. Very much in tune with each other and obviously in love. Tina gathered from their conversation that Maggie was a witch as well. Here she sat with three couples who were all madly in love. Boy did she feel like a fifth wheel, or in this case a seventh. Edna didn't bring up time travel and neither did any of the others. Maggie and Dylan were curious about the tour they'd just completed.

"Dylan loves to sing and he's got a great voice," Maggie offered.

"Do ye now?" Hamish asked.

"I do love to sing, but as for the great voice, Maggie might be a little bit prejudiced." Dylan took a sip of his beer, before wrinkling his nose at Maggie, who elbowed him in the side.

"Do ye play an instrument?" Hamish asked.

"A little guitar, but I am far from a musician. After you checked in, I took an opportunity to listen to some of your songs while I was cooking dinner. I love your stuff."

"Thank you so much," Elle said.

"You've definitely got some new fans," Maggie said.

"How are ye feeling?" Edna asked Elle.

"Pretty good. I think this might be the first meal I've been able to eat without feeling sick."

"Must be Dylan's good cooking," Edna said, a suspicious twinkle in her eyes.

Tina wondered if Edna had put some spell on Elle to keep her morning sickness at bay and a second later when Edna winked at her, she knew she had. She also got the feeling that Edna was reading her mind.

"I'm actually feeling great right now, knock on wood." Elle said as she rapped on the wooden dining table.

"I'm so happy to hear it," Edna said.

Tina glanced at Angus who seemed to be done eating and was sitting back in his chair with his arm across the back of Edna's. "You're very quiet Angus," she said.

"Aye. I've nae much to say. Edna does enough talking for the both of us," he teased.

Edna elbowed him in the ribs. "Don't let him fool ye. He talks plenty when he has something to say and I've learned over the years it's best to listen when he speaks."

Dylan and Maggie nodded their heads in agreement.

"It's true. He's a man of few words, but much wisdom," Maggie said.

"Yer making me blush," Angus said and they all laughed.

"It would take an awful lot to make ye blush," Edna said, leaning over to kiss his cheek.

Tina took in all the love at the table and began to feel a little depressed about her own situation. "Dinner was wonderful, Dylan. I'm a bit tired. I think I'll head up to bed. I could use a good night's sleep."

"Are you okay, sis?" Elle asked.

"Fine. Just tired. Good night, everyone."

Alone in her room, Tina wondered what it might be like to meet a man like her sister's husband. He wasn't your typical guy and she liked that about him. He never felt like he needed to do what all the other guys were doing. Sure, he enjoyed the sports he was learning about and he loved spending time with the guys in the band, but Elle was his priority and he made that clear to anyone who'd listen. They just don't make men like that anymore, or at least not many of them. She got into her pjs and climbed into bed, giving in to gravity and allowing her head to sink into the pillow and her body to completely relax. She wished Edna hadn't suggested time travel, because now it was all she could think about. She hadn't asked Elle too many questions about her experience. It seemed like it was a huge surprise to her, but it wouldn't be a surprise if Tina did it. She'd know it was going to happen and yet she was sure that the control freak in her would be a nervous wreck because her take charge attitude would do her absolutely no good. That didn't sit well with her. She didn't like being out of her element and she avoided it at all costs. It was like flying. She knew she had to do it, but she wished she was the one flying the plane. Tina wondered about this guy Edna had mentioned. What did he look like? Was he big and tall like Hamish? Was he handsome? The answers to those questions were unknowable unless she went back in time. It didn't matter. She wasn't doing it. She missed her family back home, missed her own bed, missed her niece and nephew. No. She was going home and that was all there was to it. She cleared her brain of the unwanted thoughts and closed her eyes only to dream of a broad shouldered man with dark hair and blue eyes.

CHAPTER 2

Breaghacraig - 1518

Donal McCabe was having a good day. He'd bested every man he'd come up against on the practice field and he was feeling very happy with himself. Head high, shoulders back and chest puffed out, Donal accepted the praise of the other warriors as they passed him on their way by. Some clapped him on the back, others, those he'd defeated, merely nodded their appreciation of his efforts. Yes, he was feeling pretty good about himself and to top it off, later in the evening, he planned to spend some time with the new kitchen maid. He couldn't remember her name, but that had never stopped him before. He'd simply call her love or lass or some other endearing term. It always worked.

"Donal," Logan approached him. "Good work with the men today. Hamish would be proud of ye. Ye've taken on his responsibilities as if they'd been yers all along."

He missed Hamish, although he didn't miss being yelled at for whatever transgression it was that Hamish thought him guilty of. He'd always known he was as good a warrior as Hamish and he was sure his old friend would agree.

"Do ye miss him?" Logan asked, a twinkle of mischief in his eyes.

"Aye. As much as I hate to admit it, I do. He was a good friend to me, even when I dinnae deserve such friendship."

"Come have dinner with us tonight. Sara has become quite a good cook." Logan threw an arm over Donal's shoulder.

"Nae. I cannae," he replied.

"We'd love to have ye." Logan gazed at him, obviously hoping to change his mind.

"Ye dinnae need to feel sad for me, Logan. I'm nae lonely. If all goes well, I'll be wooing the new kitchen maid out of her apron and into my bed this night."

Logan laughed out loud at him, giving Donal a playful shove. "Ye need a woman," Logan said.

"Are ye having trouble with yer hearing? I just told ye I've got one." Donal couldn't imagine what was so confusing about that.

"Not just for one night. Ye need a lass who'll marry ye." Logan had become a big proponent of marriage since Sara and he tied the knot. He believed every man needed a wife.

"I dinnae wish to be married. I wish to do as I please. There are a good many pretty faces about and I wish to bed as many lasses as I can. I'll think about marriage when I get old."

"Yer daft. Ye dinnae ken what yer missing." The look of disbelief on Logan's face was comical and Donal laughed.

"I do ken it and I dinnae believe I'm missing anything. I dinnae have to answer to anyone, but myself. If I had a wife," he lifted his hand and put up one finger and then the next as he counted all the reasons he didn't want a wife. "She'd want to know where I was, what I was doing, why I wasnae home early enough to suit her and I tell ye she wouldnae like the answers." He laughed. "I appreciate yer concern, but I'm no' the marrying kind."

"Alright. I'll leave ye to yer debauchery, but mark my words, some day a lass will come along who's more woman than ye ever knew ye needed or wanted. When she does, ye'll be the marrying kind."

He guffawed at this "Of one thing I am sure, that willnae happen."

"Well, *when* it does, remember I'm the one who told ye it would."

"I'm sure ye willnae allow me to forget."

The two men laughed and walked together to the well. Buckets of water were already waiting for them, placed there for their use. They splashed their faces with the water and then accepted drying cloths from Helene, who happened by just in time.

"Thank ye," Logan said.

"Yer welcome. I was just on my way to find Dougall. Have ye seen him?" she asked.

"Aye. He'll be along shortly," Donal replied.

"How are ye both this fine day?" she asked.

"Well," said Logan.

"Excellent," chimed in Donal, still feeling pride in his day's performance.

"Excellent? What wondrous feats have ye done to warrant that response?" Helene asked, tipping her head and regarding him with a scowl.

Donal didn't think Helene cared for him much. Like some of the other married ladies, she always seemed to frown a bit when she saw him. He certainly wasn't one to brag about how he spent his evenings when in mixed company, but he got the feeling that Helene knew more than she should about him. Thank goodness her husband, Dougall, and the other men appreciated him for his skill as a warrior and didn't care about such things. The women of the castle didn't approve of his penchant for wooing, not that it was any of their business. He didn't understand why they should care at all, but they certainly liked to hold it against him. Donal knew it wouldn't matter to her if he had defeated every warrior of the clan, she wouldn't give him the praise he deserved. Luckily, someone was approaching that would distract her from judging him.

"Helene! How I love seeing the most beautiful woman I ken." her husband, Dougall, kissed her cheek and her scowl immediately became a smile. She was a lovely lass, even when she frowned at him, but when she looked at Dougall her face glowed. He wondered for a moment what it would be like to have someone look at him like that. He shook the thought away before it could take hold. He wasn't after that particular look from a woman.

"Are ye hungry? I've some food waiting for ye inside," she said.

"Aye." He looked at Logan and Donal. "What are ye two doing?"

"Just discussing why Donal doesnae have a woman," Logan said.

"'Tis a good question," Helene said. "I cannae imagine why." Her voice dripped with sarcasm as she turned and walked away. The men slapped him on the back and laughed again, then Dougall followed along behind her like an obedient husband, something Donal never wanted to be. Dougall, one of the finest warriors of the Mackenzie clan was reduced to following orders from a woman. He couldn't believe it.

Donal knew Helene and the others had been poking fun at him and he didn't like it. How dare they ruin his perfect day with their judgement? "'Tis none of yer business," he called after them. "Now, if ye dinnae mind. I'm hungry." He marched off to the kitchen to see what Mary had to offer, never looking back, despite the laughter coming from Logan and some of the others who'd joined him. Why were they always trying to marry him off? It made no sense to him and never would. He was a happy man. He didn't need the same woman warming his bed every night. The smile he'd worn only moments ago had turned into an angry scowl. By the time he reached the kitchen his temper made him fling open the door at the same time as a young lass exited right into his arms.

"Oh, I'm so sorry," she said.

"Dinnae be sorry, lass. I quite enjoyed it." It was his kitchen maid. He gave her his best smile, the one that always worked. "Where are ye off to in such a hurry? I've only just arrived."

"I must go home. My mother sent word. She needs me," she extricated herself from his arms and tried to squeeze past him.

"Ye'll be back soon, I hope," he snaked his arm around her waist, holding her still so he could look into her eyes. Nothing there gave him hope.

"I dinnae ken that I will," she said, glancing back into the kitchen.

"Will ye still meet me later?" he asked, worried that this day was going from good to bad too quickly for his tastes.

"Nae. I willnae," she said with certainty.

Damn it all. "Mayhap tomorrow night then?" he hoped.

"I'm nae sure. I'll tell ye tomorrow... if I'm back." She seemed in a hurry to escape him. Maybe he should try a different tactic.

"What's wrong at home, lass? It must be something quite terrible if yer nae sure of yer return." There, he could be sensitive when it was called for.

"Ma's having her baby. I must go." She disconnected herself from his hands and ran across the courtyard. He watched as she headed off through the castle gates and out of sight.

Entering the kitchen, all hope of celebrating his victories dashed, Mary pushed a bowl of stew in front of him. "There ye go, lad."

"Thank ye, Mary."

"Ye look in quite the state," she noted.

"Aye. This day is not turning out the way I had hoped. The lass... she has to go see about her ma," he said.

"Oh, ye mean Bethia."

"Is that her name? Bethia," he repeated as if it were a foreign word. "Are ye sure? It doesnae ring a bell."

"Well, it should." She scowled at him much like Helene had. "Ye've been sniffing at her skirts for a week now. Shame on ye fer nae remembering."

Mary made him feel guilty in a way no one else could. She reminded him of his grannie. She was sweet and kind, but dinnae cross her or anyone she cared about.

"I'm sorry, Mary. Yer right. I should hae remembered."

"So, yer night's been ruined by the inconsiderate way her ma decided to have her bairn this day," Mary said. Her obvious mocking tone lost on him.

"Aye."

Mary cuffed him on the back of the head. "Ye daft oaf. What is wrong with ye?"

"I dinnae think there was anything wrong with me until today," he answered, rubbing the back of his head. The only person who understood him was Hamish and he wasn't here anymore. He'd succumbed to the lure of a woman and run off with her. He never even said goodbye.

Donal ate his stew, but didn't really enjoy it the way he usually did. Maybe it was the way Mary tsk-tsked at him as she worked.

"Oh, hello, Donal," Sophia said, entering the kitchen. "Mary, Bethia told me about her Ma and I thought ye could use some help."

"'Tis yer day off, lass." Mary wiped her brow with her apron. The warmth of the kitchen could be overwhelming at times. How Mary did it day in and day out he didn't know.

"I know, but I wasn't busy, so I'm here if you need me," Sophia said.

"I do, thank ye, lass" Mary said, breathing a sigh of relief.

"Latharn told me ye bested him today on the field," Sophia said, directing her comment to Donal as she wiped down the table he sat at.

"And I was feeling pretty good about it until now," he answered, glancing at Mary who narrowed her eyes at him.

"You should be proud. He's a tough one." She lifted his bowl and wiped under it. "He wasn't happy about it, but he said he was impressed with your skill."

"Finally, someone has something nice to say about me." His narrowed eyes were directed at Mary's back.

Sophia laughed. "Is someone feeling sorry for themselves?"

Sophia was one of the lasses that had come from the future and decided to make Breaghacraig their home. They had an odd way of speaking, forcing him to ask on more than one occasion just what it was they were talking about. In this case, he understood exactly what she was getting at. He didn't agree. He was merely baffled by the lack of respect he'd been shown by everyone he'd come across since his resounding victory on the field this morning.

～

THE THISTLE & HIVE INN - 2018

Edna's office was a cozy retreat tucked in behind the registration desk in the lobby. Tina was seated on the comfy sofa having tea with Edna and Maggie, enjoying the fact that there was absolutely nowhere she had to be and nothing she had to do. Elle and Hamish were exploring the village and she was free to enjoy her down time. The tour was over and her duties as the tour manager were also over. She had no commitments back home and had no idea what she'd be doing with her time once she got there.

"I could get used to this," Tina said.

"Why don't ye stay with us for a while?" Edna asked.

"I should," she said only half joking.

"We'd love to have ye," Maggie said. "Dylan and I can show ye around Glendaloch and the surrounding area. Ye'd love it I'm sure."

This was sounding more and more attractive to her, but Elle and Hamish were expecting her to head back home with them. She really shouldn't.

"Maggie, I was speaking with Tina about taking a little time travel journey to Breaghacraig. What do ye think?"

"Does she want to?" Maggie asked, sounding surprised and looking to Tina.

"I don't think I can. It all sounds so incredible to me, but I'm expected at home," Tina said.

"Well, don't let Auntie Edna pressure ye into anything," Maggie eyed Edna with some apparent disapproval.

"Oh, Maggie, ye ken 'tis perfectly safe," Edna protested.

"'Tis, but *we* decided we weren't going to send anyone else back against their will," Maggie replied with an arched brow.

"It wouldn't be against her will," Edna sounded a little defensive.

Tina watched the verbal ping pong match going on between aunt and niece. It seemed like such a crazy idea, but if she could find a man like Elle had, it might just be worth it. Maybe if she had a better idea of what to expect, it wouldn't be so overwhelming. Knowing exactly what was going to happen would give her the control she liked and maybe then she could think about having a little fun. "This man you say is waiting for me. What's he like?"

Edna seemed pleased with her question and shot a look of satisfaction at Maggie. She smiled brightly as she replied. "He's a good man, like Hamish, but he is a bit lost at the moment. He needs a woman in his life who can lead him in the right direction."

"So he's heading in the wrong direction?" Tina didn't like the sound of that.

"I wouldn't say it was the wrong direction, he's just a bit lost and he needs yer help."

"Help?" she asked, thinking she certainly didn't want a man who needed help.

"Aye. Ye ken how the menfolk are. They always need our help. Isnae that right, Maggie?"

Maggie looked as confused as Tina felt. "I guess."

"Ye wouldnae have to worry. Wallace will meet ye on the other side of the bridge and he'll take ye to Breaghacraig. There are several others there who have traveled through time."

"Why are they still there?" Tina wondered.

"They wanted to stay."

"I don't want to stay." She surprised them all with the vehemence in her tone, but the idea of staying somewhere like that was terrifying. She was fine with a little adventure, just not too much of one. She took a breath and controlled her emotions. "I can't stay."

"Understood, dear. I'm just telling ye that Ashley, Jenna and the other lassies would be there for ye and, of course, when yer ready to come back to present time they'll help ye get here." Edna's warm smile and compassionate eyes put her at ease. She made everything sound so easy. Tina couldn't believe it, but as crazy at it seemed, she was actually considering this!

"I don't want to condone my aunt's meddling," Maggie gave her aunt a meaningful look, "but it is a once in a lifetime chance to see a place that no longer exists, at least not on this side of the bridge."

"Have you both been there?" Tina asked.

"We have and so has Dylan," Maggie said. "No matter what ye decide. My offer still stands to take ye on a tour of the Highlands."

Tina's mind was at odds. It was so nice to be able to sit still, to not have people asking her a million questions a day. And as much as she loved her family, they had spent an awful lot of time together. A bit of time all on her own seemed like a great idea. She wasn't sure if she could really go through with traveling through time, but the idea of spending a few more days in Scotland was appealing.

"Thanks, Maggie. That's so kind of you. I haven't made up my mind about the time travel, but I'm definitely going to stay. I could use some time off."

The bell above the inn door rang, signaling someone arriving. "I'll go see who it is," Maggie said. She opened the office door and then called over her shoulder, "It's Elle and Hamish."

"Tell them to join us," Edna said.

Maggie waved them back to the office. Tina could hear her sister laughing with Hamish and as they came through the door, the look of love on both their faces made her heart happy. It also made her mind up for her. She wanted what they had and if she had to travel back in time to get it, she would. Of course, she was keeping that information to herself. She didn't want Elle to talk her out of it, or to worry about her.

"Did ye two have fun?" Edna asked, smiling brightly at the happy couple.

"We did," Elle said. "I love it here."

"Me, too," Hamish added. "Scotland is such a different place now. So much has changed, but thank goodness the whisky hasnae." Hamish chuckled at this before continuing. "I *will* be glad to get back home. I've plans to make a crib for our wee one and cannae wait to get started."

"I've got some news," Tina said, nervously fidgeting with the arm of the sofa. "I've decided to take a vacation. I'm going to stay here in Scotland. Maggie and Dylan have offered to take me on a tour of the Highlands."

"Oh, that's wonderful, Tina. You've been working so hard on this tour for so long. You deserve a nice vacation."

"Really? You don't mind?" She couldn't help but worry. What if they needed her for something on the trip home.

"Of course not. Why would I mind? I think we can manage to get ourselves home without you." Elle grasped Hamish's hand as a soft, sweet smile appeared on her lips. "We'll be fine. I promise."

"You'll explain to Mom and Dad?"

"Don't worry. I'll tell them. I'm sure they'll be happy you're taking some time for yourself."

She'd done it. She'd taken the first step. Once Elle and Hamish were gone she'd tell Edna she'd made her decision. A shiver of excitement bubbled up in her and she smiled. She was going to meet her man.

∼

The following afternoon, they saw Elle and Hamish off. She hugged and kissed them both.

"I'm so happy you're doing this, Tina. You're glowing. I mean it, I haven't seen you this happy in ages."

"I'm really looking forward to it. You two have a safe trip home and take care of my little niece," she said.

"Nephew," Hamish said. This was a debate the two of them had been having ever since they found out Elle was pregnant.

"I hope you're not disappointed when I'm right," she teased, poking him in the ribs.

He put an arm around Tina's shoulder, pulling her in to give her a hug. "I'll miss yer sassy talk," he said.

Her relationship with Hamish was one filled with teasing jabs at one another, but also genuine love. She had brothers and felt lucky to be close to them, so she never expected Hamish to worm his way into her heart the way he did. They were all very lucky to have him in their lives.

Their limo pulled up to the curb and once everyone said their goodbyes, they were off. Tina felt a sense of freedom as she watched the car drive out of sight. She'd never traveled alone before and she felt those butterflies again, something exciting was happening and she could not wait. Finally, she would be able to go somewhere on her own where no one would think of her as just Elle's sister. There were a lot of unknown factors, but for once she was willing to just embrace the adventure of it and she was feeling pretty proud of herself.

Turning to Edna, she said, "Let's talk time travel."

"Am I hearing ye right, lass? Are ye going to do this?" Edna's smile revealed she knew all along that Tina would go.

"I am. I'm a little nervous. Damn, who am I kidding? I'm a lot nervous, but I'm also excited." Her hands were shaking uncontrollably and so she tucked them under her arms.

"You won't regret it, I promise," Edna assured her.

"When will I go?" she asked. Now that she'd made up her mind, it couldn't be soon enough. She had to do it before she changed her mind.

"Tomorrow. We have to get ye some appropriate clothing to wear and I'll send ye with a basket of goodies for yer hosts. Oh, and some scones for my Wallace. I can't forget that." Edna was busy rattling off a never ending list of things Tina would bring with her. Before she knew it, she was following Edna around the little village stopping in stores for treats and snacks for her journey, and a few mystery items as well. When they were out of earshot of other shoppers, Edna would tell her about the bridge and the fog, the castle and some of the residents there. Edna kept up the commentary and then steered them back to the inn with Tina's head spinning.

When they got back she must have looked a bit dazed because Maggie only shrugged her shoulders and directed her back into the inn where Dylan and Angus were sitting at the bar having an ale. "Can I get ye something to drink, lass?" Angus asked.

"I think I'm going to need something stronger than wine tonight," Tina said taking a deep breath.

"And why would that be?"

"I'm going to time travel," she said.

Angus looked from her to his wife. "Edna! What have I told ye?"

"I ken it, Angus, but there's someone waiting for her. Ye wouldnae deny her the chance at true love, would ye?"

He let out a breath, shaking his head as he went behind the bar and pulled out a cocktail shaker. "Would ye like a martini, lass?"

"Yes, please."

"I make a good one," he assured her.

"Good. Extra olives, please?"

"Yer wish is my command," he said, bowing at the waist.

She liked Angus. They hadn't had much of a chance to get to know each other, but he had a nice calming effect on her. She imagined he did the same for Edna who seemed a high energy lady. He placed a very large martini on the bar, winking at her as he did.

Tina hoped it was going to relax her enough so she could sleep later.

"Enjoy yer drink. I'm going to prepare yer things for the trip," Edna said.

"I'm sure ye already know this, but just in case, ye won't need yer suitcase or yer phone. They'll be of no use to ye there," Maggie said.

"Oh, okay," Tina replied. She hadn't really thought about the fact that she would be cut off from everything and everyone. "I'm leaving this all up to you and Edna. Whatever you say goes." That was not how she usually operated and she could feel the panic starting to build inside her. "You know, I'm used to always being the one taking care of everyone else's travel plans, it's nice to leave it all to someone else."

There must have been something off about her voice because Angus reached over and patted her arm kindly, "Edna will take good care of ye lass. There is nothing to worry about." And just like that, she felt the panic subside. She didn't know if Angus was magic, too, but there was definitely something calming in the touch of his giant hand.

She raised her glass in a toast and the others did the same. "To time travel."

CHAPTER 3

Scotland - 1518

She'd done it. She'd traveled through time, through the fog and now she was seated next to a very happy Wallace.

"Edna said you loved those scones. She asked me to make sure you got them," Tina said, placing the bag of scones on the wooden bench between them.

"Thank ye, lass. She's right. I look forward to them with great relish."

They started off down the path into the surrounding woods. The smell of pine scented trees tickled her nose with their delightful scent. Birds chirped happily from their perches up high and she thought how this wasn't much different from her own time. She glanced over at Wallace, who despite his clothing looked very real. She wasn't sure what she had expected him to look like, but his kind eyes and happy smile assured her all would be well. "Did you take my sister to Breaghacraig, Wallace?" she asked.

"Nae. Hamish brought her."

She hadn't heard that part of their story. She looked around them, wondering if the man she was supposed to meet would be meeting them soon. Edna had said Wallace would take her to Breaghacraig, but hadn't said when or where she would meet her mystery man. Wallace was friendly enough, but not as chatty as Edna. She thought for a while about a topic they could cover. "Do you do this often?"

"Whenever Edna needs me." He smiled reassuringly at her.

"How does she get in touch with you?" she asked.

"Through the fire. I cannae say that I'm used to it yet, but 'tis how she communicates with me."

"When you say through the fire, what do you mean?" she couldn't even begin to imagine.

"Through my hearth, ye ken." He said it as if she should know exactly what he was talking about.

"Oh, I see," she lied.

"Ye'll see. If she needs to talk to ye, she may do the same." He continued to guide the cart down the wooded path.

"Wow! I'm glad you told me because otherwise I'd probably freak out." She thought she probably would anyway. That seemed a crazy way to talk to someone, but wasn't this whole thing crazy?

"Lass, I dinnae understand the way ye speak. I dinnae ken 'freak out.'"

Tina laughed. "I guess you wouldn't. I just mean I'd probably be scared."

"That I understand and the first time she spoke to me I, as ye say, freaked out."

She laughed again. He'd put her quite at ease and their journey to Breaghacraig was no longer as scary as she thought it would be when she'd stepped across the bridge. This was definitely doable. She'd just pretend she was vacationing at a medieval theme park. That should help and when she got to Breaghacraig, she'd meet her man and be on her way back home in no time. She settled into her seat and took in the sights. In some ways, the scenery they passed seemed similar to Livermore. Throw in a winery or two and it could be. She wondered what her sister had been thinking as she made this journey. She'd have to remember to ask her when she got back home. She'd told Elle she was going on a tour of the Highlands and so she was. She just hadn't said what century she'd be touring in.

"Ye seem like a happy lass," Wallace observed as he drove his horse up to a ground eating trot.

"You know, I am happy. I'm looking forward to seeing what the future holds for me."

"So ye dinnae ken it?" he asked.

"No. Should I?" Did he know something she didn't?

"Nae," he said, not offering anything else.

"Did Edna tell you anything about the man I'm supposed to meet?" she asked. Her curiosity was getting the better of her.

"I'm afraid she didnae." He just shook his head at her and turned back to the horse.

"Okay. It just kind of sounded like you might know something." Tina felt the panic wanting to resurface again. She took a deep breath and reminded herself that this was an adventure, she closed her eyes and blew out the breath and felt the panic start to dissipate.

"Lass, as I've said. I dinnae ken much of what ye say. I probably misunderstood ye. Now, settle back. We've got a long way to go, but dinnae fear I haven't lost a lass yet."

Tina tensed up in her seat until she noticed Wallace winking at her. "Wallace! I'm surprised at you!"

He chuckled. "I like ye, lass. I think I'm going to enjoy this."

~

The day started off with such promise, as had the day before and the day before that. Those had ended poorly for him, but Donal hoped that today might end differently. The lass in the kitchen was back and she'd agreed to meet him by the postern gate at sunset. If all went well, he'd be exactly where he wished to be, in the arms of a beautiful, buxom red-haired lass. The mere thought of it set his pulse to racing and his kilt to rising. He spun quickly leaning on the well to hide his more than obvious arousal at the thought of Bess... Beth... Oh, what was her name? He nodded to the few passersby who gave him curious stares as he ran names through his head determined to get it right. "Bethia!" he exclaimed out loud, slamming his palm into his forehead. How was it that he couldn't for the life of him remember it.

"Donal? Did ye call me," Bethia asked, approaching the well with an empty bucket.

"Och! Aye. Aye. I did."

She smiled sweetly at him as she lowered her bucket into the well.

"Here. Allow me to help ye with that," he said. No one would ever accuse him of nae being chivalrous. She moved out of the way as he hoisted the now filled bucket up and set it on the ledge of the well.

"What did ye want?" she asked.

"I wished to tell ye how beautiful ye…" Bethia didnae seem to be listening to him. He was trying to woo her a bit and instead she was glancing towards the gate.

Turning his head to see what was so fascinating, he noted an elderly couple speaking with the guard, who glanced around and upon seeing Donal pointed in his direction.

"Who are they?" Bethia asked, standing so close to his side that his arm brushed her breast.

He fought to control his erection as the couple approached. "I dinnae recognize them," he said. He turned towards her and his arm again brushed her breast. Tonight was definitely going to be better than the last.

"Are ye Donal?" the elderly man shouted as he got closer.

Donal was startled at the man's angry tone. He turned to give him his full attention, "Aye," he answered. He looked from the man to the woman and back not recognizing these people.

"We've something for ye," he said, motioning to the woman who was carrying something.

"For me?" What could it be? He hoped it was something good.

"Aye. 'Tis yers," the man practically hissed at him.

The woman raised a plaid wrapped package with shaky arms and placed it into his hands. As soon as she did, it began to wriggle and shriek.

"What's this?" he asked, a look of horror on his face.

Bethia peeked into the blankets.

"'Tis a bairn," she said. The look she gave him was one he would never forget. Shock and something else rested there. Accusation.

"Why do ye give me yer bairn?" he stuttered out.

"She's yers," the woman said, her voice choked with tears.

"I dinnae understand. I have nae child." These people were daft.

"Ye do now," the old man said. He motioned to his wife and they began to walk away.

He glanced at Bethia, who was shaking her head in apparent disbelief. She picked up her bucket and turned away from him.

"Bethia. Dinnae leave. The bairn isnae mine." He scrambled after the couple. "Wait. Take her back. She isnae mine."

The man turned and pointed a crooked finger at Donal's chest, "Ye soiled our daughter," he yelled and all of Donal's blood drained from his body. He was suddenly very cold and very still. "And now that she's gone…" he stopped and clenched his jaw for moment before continuing, "we cannae care for this wee one. Yer her Da. 'Tis yer duty to care for her."

"Gone?" He looked to the old woman, but she would not meet his eyes. "Is she dead?" he asked.

"Aye, the fever took her from us." The fight had gone out of the man and somehow, he looked even older than he did before. "She hadnae been well since the birth. We held out hope she would regain her strength, but then she fell ill. We dinnae have the means to care for the child. She's yers now." He turned and started walking away again.

Donal watched him take a few steps, his mind racing and he realized, he didn't know who the man was talking about. "Wait. I dinnae ken who yer daughter is. Please tell me." He hadn't been so panicked at any point in his life, even in the heat of battle.

"Her name was Sionaid. Sionaid MacGregor."

The woman wept silently as they marched away from him. He watched them head toward the gate and just stood there. The child had stopped shrieking at some point and he looked at her to try and make sense of this.

"Sionaid." Blast his faulty memory.

"Do ye nae remember her?" Bethia asked.

He didn't know when she had walked up beside him, but she'd obviously heard enough of the man's story to know what happened. "Nae. I dinnae."

"Shame on ye. Ye lout." He looked up at her suddenly and saw sparks of anger glowing in her eyes. "She was one of the kitchen maids."

"When?" This couldn't be happening to him. They must be mistaken. Maybe if he hurried he could catch them and give the bairn back.

"She hasnae been here for well over a year." She took her bucket and began to walk away from him.

"Will I see ye at the postern gate?" he asked, knowing deep in his heart what the answer would be.

She turned on her heel and came back, one finger poking him right in the chest, "Ye are a daft fool if ye think that I, or any lass here would ever meet ye again." She turned back and was soon out of sight. He hurried towards the gates, his eyes scanning the many people going about their daily chores, coming and going through the gate. He couldn't find them.

He approached the guard, "The people who were looking for me, where did they go?"

"They got in their wagon and left. I wouldnae have thought their old nag would go that fast, but they were certainly in a hurry," he answered. The bairn wiggled and nearly fell out of his arms. "What have ye there, Donal? The fruits of yer labor?" The man chuckled and Donal vowed that once he had this straightened out he'd be back to land a solid blow to the guard's protruding nose.

Just outside the castle gates, all he could see were the crowds of people coming and going from market day. There were carts, horses and throngs of people. So many that he'd be lucky to find the man and woman who'd just ruined his life.

He didn't believe curses truly existed, but the way the last few days had gone he could be convinced of it. He headed back to the courtyard, awkwardly holding the bundle he'd been handed. Securing the bairn in one arm, he used his other hand to move the plaid to find a very unhappy wee one staring out at him, tears spilling from her eyes, face red from all the angry screaming she'd been doing.

"What is yer name? They didnae even tell me that." His heart sank. How is it that he'd never, ever given a thought to one of the many women he'd been with having his bairn? Bethia was right. He was a daft fool.

"What have we here?" Cormac's voice forced him to look up from the babe.

He found he was unable to speak.

Cailin, Logan, Robert and Dougall joined Cormac fresh from the practice field. He was surrounded by men he counted as his brothers, but he was too stunned to speak. A cry from the bundle drew all their eyes and he watched as each man realized what he was holding.

"Is the bairn yers?" Cailin asked.

"So I've been told," he muttered. Donal had never shied away from sharing his conquests with them, but now he worried what they would think. He had been careless and now there was a bairn without a mother. It was all his fault and he didn't know what these men would think of him. For the first time since arriving at the castle, he feared that they would turn him out. It was no less than he deserved.

"Who's the mother and where is she?" Dougall asked.

Robert reached into the bundle and touched the bairn's face, tracing her eye brows and down her nose. She immediately quieted and reached for his hand. "That would be my question as well," he added.

Donal focused on the bairn, it was easier than looking up to see the disappointment he knew would be in their eyes. "She was a kitchen maid here. I didnae ken she was with child. She didnae tell me." She must have understood what a poor excuse for a father he'd be and thought better of it. "She's passed and her Ma and Da brought the bairn to me."

They were silent and Donal felt the heaviness on his shoulders. He tried his best to remember what Sionaid looked like. If she was the lass he was thinking of, she was quite pretty with blonde locks and emerald green eyes. He was ashamed of himself. So wrapped up in his own conquests that he never thought this might happen. He hadn't mean to hurt anyone. He had been so careless. What a sorry excuse for a man.

"I dinnae wish to say anything about yer skills in the Da department, but this wee one needs a Ma," Robert said. "I'll send condolences to her family. I'm hoping Mary kens who they are."

"What will I do?" The helpless feeling in his gut was growing to the point where he thought he might be sick. He gazed at the screaming bairn in his arms.

"Ye must rock her a bit," Cailin said, swaying back and forth. "Like this."

Donal felt like a fool, but he did as Cailin suggested and was pleased that after a moment or two the babe quieted. They were not throwing him out and that small bit of reassurance allowed him to look up into their eyes.

"Here, wipe her tears and her nose," Cormac said, handing him a kerchief.

Again, Donal did as he was told. "She's a pretty wee one," he said, a bit of pride slipping into his voice.

"Aye. She must take after her mother." Dougall chuckled, placing a hand on Donal's shoulder.

The group of Highlanders gathered around the wee lass, cooing at her and doing their best to make her smile. Donal wasn't sure how he would manage, but knowing that his friends were by his side made him feel a wee bit better.

~

Wallace guided the wagon into the inner courtyard of Breaghacraig. The tall stone walls of the castle were formidable, stretching up high into the bright blue of the sky. Smaller buildings lined the walls of the courtyard, housing a blacksmith, stables and other things she couldn't name. Tina was awestruck by the sight of it. She felt a bit overwhelmed as it reconfirmed that she was in the sixteenth-century. The people they passed nodded to Wallace as he brought the wagon to a stop in front of two large wooden doors.

"It seems we've arrived just in time," Wallace said, nodding towards the group of men huddled together.

"What are they doing?" she asked. They appeared to be focused on something one of the men was holding. "Is that a baby?"

"I believe 'tis," Wallace said.

She had no idea who the man was that she was supposed to meet, but the group she was seeing were all very handsome. "Is one of them the man I'm here for?"

"I dinnae ken, lass. Edna has told me verra little." He got down from the wagon and came around to her side to help her down.

"So, she's told you *something*," Tina said hoping he'd divulge any information he may have.

Wallace rolled his eyes in his head. "She told me to bring ye here. 'Tis all I know."

"Are you going to leave me? I don't know what to do." Panic crept into her voice at the thought of navigating her way here in this foreign land and ancient time. She must have been out of her mind thinking she could do this. This was no vacation. This was real.

"Don't worry. There are many here who will help ye," Wallace assured her, holding her hands. His kind eyes held her gaze almost willing her to relax.

One of the handsome men was walking towards them. He was quite tall with long black hair and even from a distance she could see his amazing blue eyes. She straightened her dress and checked her hair as he approached. "Wallace, welcome! I see ye've brought us another lass. I assume she's been sent by Edna."

"Ye assume correctly, sir. This is Tina. She is the sister to Elle." He released one hand as he presented her to this gorgeous man. Her breath caught in her throat as she tried to speak.

"Ah. Ye do resemble her. How is our Hamish?" the man asked.

"He's great," Tina said, finally finding her voice.

"Pardon my rudeness, I should introduce myself. I be Robert

Mackenzie, laird of the clan. We've many a lass from yer time here with us. I imagine ye'll be wanting to speak with them."

"I'd like that," Tina responded.

"Well, come with me, lass." He held his arm out for her to take. "Thank ye, Wallace. Mary will be pleased to see ye."

Wallace bowed to Robert and turned to Tina. "Good luck to ye, lass."

"Thank you, Wallace. You were wonderful company," she said, truly meaning every word of it.

He turned and walked away leaving her feeling a bit awkward and nervous. How lucky was she? Robert wasn't only handsome, he was the laird.

"Shall we?" Robert asked.

She blushed and nodded. Robert led her through the heavy doors and into an expansive room, which she imagined was the great hall Edna had told her about. A beautiful dark-haired woman met them and Robert introduced her.

"This is me wife, Irene," he said.

Tina's heart sank. She'd been mistaken. Robert was already taken. "Tina," she said, holding her hand out to Irene.

Irene took her hand and patted it as she held it. "Welcome to Breaghacraig," she said.

"Thank you."

"Irene, Edna sent her. She's Elle's sister," Robert explained.

She hadn't even been here five minutes and she was already back to being Elle's sister. Some things never changed.

"Will ye get Ashley? She's with the children upstairs," Irene said.

"Of course," Robert said, leaving Tina's side. "I'll send her right down."

"Come, sit," Irene said

Tina was too nervous to sit right away, so she took a moment to ground herself by looking around the room. The hearth was larger than any she'd ever seen in her life. The opening was as tall as she was. Over the top was a beautiful tapestry of mostly greens and golds, but with many other colors throughout. It depicted the castle in the center surrounded by water on one side and trees on the other. Birds were sprinkled here and there in the sky over the water and seated in the trees. Several ornate wooden chairs were placed in a semi-circle around the hearth, where a small fire burned. She tried to keep her mind from wandering to how crazy this all was. Maybe she'd made a mistake. It might not be too late to find Wallace and have him take her back to the bridge.

"Are ye hungry?" Irene asked, interrupting her muddled thoughts.

"No. Wallace and I ate not too long ago. He's very nice," she felt herself beginning to babble and tried to get a grip on herself. "How many women from my time are there here?"

"Let's see. There's Ashley, Jenna, Sophia, and Sara. I think that's all of them," she laughed. Tina spun in her seat to look at her, surely she didn't hear her right. That many modern women had chosen to live in the past?

"Are they all married to men they met here?" she asked.

"Aye. They'll tell ye all about it. Ye seem nervous," Irene observed.

"I guess I'm not doing a very good job of hiding it, am I." She rested her hand on her belly, feeling sick.

"If I were in yer shoes, I'd be much the same," Irene assured her.

Tina took a deep breath in an attempt to calm her nerves. She glanced around the hall. "This is so beautiful," she said. "I feel like I'm in a museum."

"Hmmm..." Irene responded seeming unsure of what Tina was saying.

"I mean, I know it's not a museum, but it's just so perfect."

"Thank ye." Irene took her by the arm and led her to a chair. "Sit. Helene!" she called.

A moment later a very pregnant blonde woman entered the hall. "Aye. Ye called?"

"Helene, this is Tina. She's Elle's sister. Edna has sent her to us and I think she needs a dram."

Helene tipped her head examining Tina, who was feeling uncomfortable under her scrutiny.

"I believe 'tis so," Helene said. She left the room and returned only a moment later carrying an oddly shaped vessel.

"What's this?" Tina asked.

"A wee bit of whisky. It settles the nerves. Drink," Helene said.

She wasn't sure she wanted a drink, but then again, her nerves were starting to get the better of her and if these two ladies who didn't even know her could tell, then she should probably take the drink. She took the vessel in her hands. It had two flat handles on either side of a small wooden cup. Before she could give it too much thought, she downed the entire contents of the cup. It burned as it headed down to her belly, but the warmth once it got there was soothing.

Irene and Helene exchanged amused looks and then glanced back to Tina. "Better?" Irene asked.

"I think so," she answered.

"Hello." A very pretty, petite woman entered the hall and made her way right to Tina. "I'm Ashley. Tina, right?"

"Yes. I'm so happy to meet you," Tina gushed.

"I'm sure you've got lots of questions. Don't worry. I've got most of the answers," she smiled warmly putting Tina at ease.

"I'll go see that her chamber is ready," Helene said.

"Thank ye, Helene," Irene said. "I'll leave ye both. Ye'll have much to speak of."

"It was lovely meeting you, Irene," Tina said as Irene left the room. She wasn't even out of the room when a commotion at the entrance drew their attention. "What's going on?"

"I don't know. Let's find out," Ashley said.

They were about to head to the doors when the group of men she'd seen outside entered.

"Cailin, what's going on?" she asked.

"Donal is a father," Cailin said.

"What?" She seemed quite shocked by this pronouncement.

"Aye. The babe's grandda and granny brought her."

The apparent father stood in the center of the men a shocked expression on his face.

"This is my husband, Cailin," Ashley said, introducing her. "This is Tina. She's Elle's sister."

The one holding the baby perked up. "Hamish," he said.

"Yes. Elle is married to Hamish," Tina said. She wasn't sure what was going on or why this man had a baby he obviously didn't know what to do with, but that wasn't any of her concern. She was here to find a husband and he definitely wasn't it.

"Is he well?" the man asked.

"Well and happy," she answered, looking at the other three men with him. She knew Cailin was taken, so trying not to be too obvious, she snuck a peek at each of them.

Ashley must have read her like a book. "This is Dougall," she said pointing to the blonde man. "He's Helene's husband. Cormac is Cailin's brother, he's married to Jenna and Logan is married to Sara."

So, they were all spoken for, except the one holding the baby.

"And this is Donal," she said, a note of disapproval in her voice.

"Ashley, would ye like to hold the wee lass?" he asked, holding the baby out to her. There was something in his voice that almost sounded like pleading.

"What's her name?" Ashley wondered.

"I dinnae ken it. They didnae tell me. She was put in me arms and they walked away. Can ye believe it?" He placed the baby into Ashley's outstretched arms, seeming relieved to hand her off to someone else.

The poor guy's in shock, Tina thought. It tore at her heart that this baby was just abandoned like that. What kind of place was this?

"What's her mother's name?" Ashley asked.

"Her Ma has passed, but her name was Sionaid."

"Then that's what ye should call her." She tickled the child under her chin, smiling at her. "Would ye like that, sweetie? She looks to be about ten months old."

Donal shrugged. He apparently knew nothing, which didn't bode well for this little one.

"Of course, if ye have another name ye prefer, you could call her that," Ashley said.

"I've not one." He looked at Tina. "Not yet."

"Well, think on it. And, Donal, don't worry. We'll help ye care for her. None of this is her fault."

Again, Tina noted the tone Ashley was using with him and she wondered why this woman didn't care for him.

"Cailin, he'll need to sleep somewhere other than the soldier's barracks. We can't have this sweet little one sleeping with all those smelly men, can we?"

"We'll find ye a room here in the castle for now. Ye'll need a cottage of yer own so ye can raise her proper," Cailin added.

Donal looked as if he might collapse right there on the spot. "He looks like he needs to sit down," Tina noted.

"I'd have to agree," Ashley said. "Donal, here, sit."

"Thank ye, Lady Ashley." Tina couldn't believe that the grandparents would just leave a baby here like this. Tina's mother and father would never have done that. She took a good look at the little one for the first time. "Hi, sweetie," she said, placing her finger in the baby's hand. "I'm so sorry about your mother." She received a giggle for her efforts. "Aren't you adorable?"

"Would you mind holding her for a minute?" Ashley asked.

"You don't have to ask twice," Tina took the baby and cradled her like a pro. "My brother has kids and Elle's expecting."

"Hamish will be a Da?" Donal said, a certain amount of astonishment in his voice.

"He will. Like you." Tina's heart ached for Donal. He'd lost his wife and now he found himself with a child to care for. He seemed ill-equipped. "This must be hard for you," Tina said. "Losing your wife and all." She had no idea how things worked here. She guessed because he was a soldier that he didn't live at home with his wife. Maybe it was one of those arranged marriages she had read about. He looked so lost, her heart went out to him.

CHAPTER 4

Donal's luck hadn't been the best of late, but it seemed things might be changing a wee bit in his favor. This lass could be the answer to his as yet unsaid prayers. She seemed to know something about bairns and was quite sympathetic to his plight. Perhaps he could convince her to take the wee lass she held in her arms. A twinge of guilt hit him as he rose from the chair and approached Tina, but he couldn't let that stop him. It was what would be best for the wee one and for himself.

"What would ye name her?" he asked, inhaling an unfamiliar perfumed scent as he lowered his head so it was right next to hers. He gazed down at the babe. He'd never paid much attention to bairns before, so it was with some surprise that he noticed how small she was. His large hand seemed almost too big to touch her wee face, but instead he reached out one finger as he'd observed Robert doing and traced her forehead, nose and cheeks down to her sweet, wee chin.

"Hmmm... I'd have to think about it. You don't want to name her after her mother?"

The question was laced with pity and he thought it possible to use it to his advantage. "I couldnae possibly name her after her Ma,

JENNAE VALE

'twould hurt too much to say her name." He hitched his breath as if holding back a sob.

He glanced around at the others who were all looking at him with varying degrees of disbelief. Luckily the lass hadn't noticed.

"You poor thing," she turned her head to see his face and he was so close her lips almost touched his. She pulled back away from him. "I'm sorry."

"Dinnae apologize. 'Twas my fault. I was standing too close. 'Tis that I wished to see the wee bairn so content in yer arms." The lass smiled, revealing sweet dimples. She was quite lovely.

Cailin cleared his throat and once he had Donal's attention, shook his head at him, before speaking. "Ye stay here with yer daughter, Donal. The rest of us have things to attend to." Cailin turned to Ashley. "I'll be back for the evening meal." He took her chin in his hand and placed a gentle kiss on her lips. Ashley took Cailin's hand in hers and they walked to the door followed by Dougall, Cormac and Logan.

"Ye seem quite motherly, lass." He wasn't lying to soften her heart. He meant it. She seemed quite at ease with the wee one, but she was a lass, of course she would be.

"I love little ones," she replied, smiling down at the bairn. "You look like you could use a bath and some clean clothes," she cooed to the baby.

"I've got some things upstairs she can wear," Ashley said, joining them. "I'll go get them and I'll arrange to have some water warmed for a bath. I'll be right back."

Left alone with Tina and the babe, Donal turned on the charm. "So, yer Elle's sister. Do ye sing?" he asked.

Tina rolled her eyes, he got the idea that she didn't like that question, "Only to myself," she said.

"The bairn may like to hear ye." He made some funny faces at the babe and when his eyes returned to Tina's face, she was looking at him with a mixture of pity and kindness.

"You're going to have to give her a name. We can't keep calling her the bairn," she observed.

"I agree. What shall we call ye, sweetling?" Almost without thinking, he took the babe from Tina's arms and cradled her, searching her face and wondering what name might suit her. She smiled up at him, melting his heart as he placed his finger in her hand. He was amazed at her strength as she pulled on it. Of course she was strong, she was his daughter. That thought brought an unexpected surge of pride and a tiny bit of peace to him. This was his daughter, his responsibility and he would do his best to take care of her. He turned his attention back to Tina, who seemed to be lost in thought. With the right woman by his side, perhaps this very one, he could be a good Da. Not a Da like his own had been. His had never paid much attention to Donal or his brothers and sisters. He wanted to be a Da like Robert or the brothers. They were strong warriors, with beautiful wives from the future. They seemed as comfortable spending time with their bairns as a woman did and still commanded respect from the men.

Tina sat in the chair by the hearth and Donal placed the little one in her lap. She bounced her up and down on her knee until the wee lass giggled uncontrollably.

"She really is sweet and happy," Tina said. He watched as she looked up, obviously thinking. "I've got it. I've been helping Elle come up with names for her baby when it's born, so I've been looking at all the baby name books."

He nodded, eager to hear what she would say and surprised to hear there were such things as baby name books.

"I keep thinking what a happy baby she is, but more than that when I look into her eyes, she has a wisdom there, like she's an old soul. She knows things. What about Elena? It means shining light or bright one."

"'Tis good," he nodded. Tina was right. It was the perfect name for his daughter. He squatted down in front of them, gazing into his daughter's face. He'd never placed much importance on names, but he could see it was crucial to give a bairn a proper name. Tina had chosen well. "Elena... Elena McCabe."

"Do you like it?" she asked, seeming unsure of herself. "I'm sure she'll be a shining light in your life."

"Aye. She will be Elena."

"And what do you think, little Elena?" she questioned the babe.

"Mama," Elena said.

The lass seemed startled. "Oh, my."

"She called ye mama," Donal said. "She thinks yer her Ma."

"I doubt that," Tina said.

"Mama," Elena repeated.

"Well, that's okay. She'll find out soon enough I'm not her Mama." She turned Elena to face Donal. "Who's that?" she asked.

"Can ye say Da?" Donal asked.

Elena let loose with a stream of unrecognizable words in reply.

"Da," Donal said again.

"Da," she repeated.

"Aye. I'm yer Da!" She'd called him Da. After a moment of elation, he sobered. He was fooling himself. He couldn't be her Da. He had no room in his life for a bairn or a wife.

"Is something wrong?" Tina asked.

He shook his head, sitting down across from her.

"Something is definitely wrong. This has got to be such a shock to you."

It was, but not for the reason she thought.

"I can't imagine how you must be feeling right now. Finding out your wife is dead and her parents just leaving you with the baby out of the blue. Why would they do that?"

"She's my bairn," was all he could manage to muster.

"Of course. And that's got to be why they left her, but you would think they would have stayed for a while. You know, to help you out until you could get Elena settled."

"What will I do?" he asked, his eyes pleading with her for help.

"I don't know," she answered.

"Could ye help me? She seems to like ye."

Tina's eyes went wide and he knew he had overstepped. "I won't be here for long." She wouldn't look at him and began rubbing her hands on her skirt. He needed to fix this. He was going to mess everything up. He had to fix this for Elena, for both of them.

He thought he had it all figured out, but this lass was only here for a brief visit. Her sad eyes touched his heart. He shouldn't impose on her. He was sure she would have helped him if she were staying.

"I'm sorry."

He sincerely believed she was. There was something about this lass. He wasn't quite sure what it was, but he found himself drawn to her.

"'Tis my worry, nae yers," he said. "Truly."

"You'll need to get settled and find someone who can help you while you're doing whatever it is that you do around here."

"I'm a soldier to clan MacKenzie," he said, "and proud to be."

"I'm sure that's important. Are you away much? Will you need someone to live with you?"

"I'll have to find someone to stay with her during the day and when I am out on patrol. What I need is a wife," he said the words while silently denying them.

"You just lost your wife. It's probably too soon to be looking for a new one," she observed.

He winced at that and hoped she would think it was his grief. "Yer right."

"Are there any older women in the clan who could take on a grandmotherly role?"

"I dinnae ken. I've never noticed." He hadn't. Why would he? He preferred the younger women and until now they'd seemed to prefer him. Once word got out about Sionaid, he'd be lucky if he ever found another woman to warm his bed.

Ashley returned with an armful of clothes. "Em's outgrown these." She handed them to Donal. "This should do her for a while. I've got the bath set up for her in my chamber." She stood, hands on her hips waiting.

Tina rose. "We've named her Elena," she said.

"Oh, that's pretty," Ashley observed.

"You should come with us, Donal. You'll need to know how to bathe and dress her," Ashley said.

Panic seized him. He didn't know the first thing about bathing a bairn and Ashley knew it. He was a warrior, and a brave one at that, but something about his wee daughter put the fear of God into him. He felt the walls closing in around him. He needed some air. "I've got some work to do. If ye wouldnae mind, I'll be back a little later." He began backing towards the entryway.

"We'll take good care of her," Tina said. "Say goodbye to Da."

Donal waved to her and then realized he was leaving with the clothes he'd just been handed. "Ye'll need these," he said as he handed the clothes back to Ashley.

"Don't you want to kiss her before you leave?" Tina asked.

He had a lot to learn about bairns. He had no idea you were supposed to kiss them when ye left. He bent down and gave her a tiny kiss on her soft cheek. "Goodbye, sweetling. Da will see ye later this day."

Upstairs in Ashley's room, they placed Elena in a shallow wash basin where Ashley took over the bathing responsibilities as Tina watched with keen interest. Things here didn't seem too different. She knew they'd had to heat up the water for the bath, which was not what she was used to, but there was a sweet smelling soap and a cloth for washing her as well. "Is that lavender I smell?"

"Yes. Isn't it heavenly? We grow our own here at the castle and the soaper makes it for us. She makes an absolutely divine pine scented soap that Cailin uses. I love the smell of it on him." She closed her eyes, inhaling as if she could smell it in this moment. "Don't worry, I'll show you all the toiletries you'll be using while you're here. You'll be clean and smelling sweet the whole time."

There was a knock at the door before it opened to reveal another young woman. "Hi." she said.

"Jenna, come in. This is Tina. She's Elle's sister."

Jenna crossed the room, hand outstretched for Tina to take. "Nice to meet you. What brings you to Breaghacraig, as if I couldn't guess," she laughed. "And who's this?"

"This is Elena," Ashley answered. "Donal's daughter."

"I didn't know he had a daughter," Jenna said, "but then again there's a lot I don't know." She grabbed a large cloth from the back of an oversized chair near the window. "Here, you look like you're about done."

"Thanks," Ashley wrapped Elena up in the towel and handed her to Tina.

"So, tell me, how's Elle?" Jenna asked. "We are all, or should I say were, huge fans of her music."

"We're still fans," Ashley corrected. "I only wish we could hear some of her new songs."

"Wouldn't that be amazing? She gave us a little concert here in the great hall," Jenna said.

"That must have been nice," Tina said, feeling for all the world like she was still living in Elle's shadow. She thought for sure that here in medieval Scotland she'd at least get a break from the constant adulation aimed at her sister. Elle deserved it, of course, but for as long as Tina could remember people were only interested in her as long as she could introduce them to Elle, or get them tickets to her concerts. Every boyfriend she'd ever had in high school, or thought she'd had, and every friend was only interested in her because of Elle. It had frustrated her then and it still did to this day, although she was trying really hard not to let it. Now here she was faced with it again, but in a different way.

"Sara will be so excited!" Ashley said. "She's an even bigger fan, if you can believe it."

"Oh, I can believe it," she hoped her tone didn't give away her true feelings. Elle was her sister and she loved her dearly, but there was always that feeling of not measuring up. The sense that no one outside of her family really cared about her, that if she were in the same room with Elle, no one would even see her. She'd be invisible. The sound of Elena's sweet babbling drew her back from her dive down the rabbit hole of self pity. Ashley and Jenna were focused on Elena and so it was now or never for Tina to shake herself free and join the conversation again.

"Elle's pregnant," she said to Jenna.

"How exciting! I'll bet Hamish is over the moon."

"Pretty much. He's so cute with her. Treats her like he's afraid she's going to break," she explained.

"Once he sees the whole birth process, he may rethink that."

The women all laughed.

"Well, I just wanted to come say hi. I've got to go check on my little guy. He was napping, but it's about time for him to wake up. Then we're going to go visit a few of the village elders. I'll see you tonight," she said to Tina as she left.

"This is so weird," Tina said. "I know I've time traveled, but meeting you and Jenna…"

"I hear ya," Ashley laughed. "We look the part, but we bring a lot of our twenty-first centuryisms with us."

"You all live here in the castle?" Tina asked.

"We do. It's nice. We've all got each other to count on." She wrapped Elena snuggly in the cloth Jenna had handed her.

"One big happy family," Tina observed.

"Sounds cliché, but it's true."

"I like that. We've got a big family and we all live in the same house. It is not as big as the castle, of course. Elle and Hamish live right next door, so we're all under each others' noses all the time."

"We are, too, I suppose, but it is more fun than I thought it would be. Jenna and I have been friends forever, we were practically sisters before ending up here, so it just feels right to be raising our kids together. Which bridge did you come by way of?" Ashley asked as she leaned in to kiss Elena's cheek.

"Glendaloch."

"That's the way I got here, too."

"If I hadn't experienced it, I'd never believe it," Tina said.

They dressed Elena in a beautiful blue velvet dress.

"Don't you look pretty?" Tina asked of wee Elena.

"It looks like it was made for her," Ashley said.

"Did you make this?" Tina asked, realizing there wasn't a mall down the street to buy baby clothes from.

"I sure did. I make all their clothes."

"Wow! I know how to thread a needle, but that's about it."

"If you live in this time, you do what you have to do. No modern conveniences."

"I guess not," Tina said. "Do you miss them? The modern conveniences?"

"Sometimes. I think the thing I miss the most is a hot shower."

"Yeah. That would be a tough one for me."

"I take it you're not planning on staying here."

"No. I couldn't leave my family. I'm only here for the experience." *And to find my man.*

～

Donal walked outside into the bright sunshine and stood there feeling lost. The courtyard was crowded with people rushing to and fro, but he hardly noticed them. He wanted to run, but where and why? Escaping his current situation would be easy enough, but it would hardly be the right thing to do. His head was spinning with thoughts of Sionaid, or the lass he thought she must have been, little Elena and how, above all else, he was going to get out of this mess. The lass Tina could be the perfect solution to his problem. He could see if she'd be interested in raising Elena as her own, leaving him to go back to life the way he liked it, without responsibility. Or, he could marry her. He'd have a wife to care for his daughter and a woman to share his bed. All this thinking was giving him a headache. He needed a drink.

He headed back to the barracks. He might as well get his clothes. He'd be staying in the castle. That was a boon he hadn't expected.

"Donal, I hear yer a Da," Marcas laughed, joined by Tam and Jock.

"I am. I dare ye to saying anything more of it." It riled him that word had already spread to the men and that they thought his situation so funny, but he knew if it were one of them in his spot, he'd do the same.

"Where are ye going?" Tam asked.

"I'm staying in the castle with the bairn." He knew that would get them.

"Aye?" The joy they seemed to find in his misfortune disappeared. "How long will they let ye stay?"

"I cannae say. I'll have to find me own croft and someone to care for wee Elena." Once again, it hit him as if he'd run headlong into the castle walls. He was a Da. Would his life ever be the same? "There's a lass just arrived. I plan to marry her. She'll care for the bairn and I can go about my life as if nary a thing has changed." He had no idea whether any of that would ever work, but he wanted these oafs to believe it would.

Once alone in his room, he reached under the bed to find the flask of whisky he kept there. He needed a swig to settle his nerves. He was as fearless as they came in battle, but the thought of *his* wee bairn put fear in his heart like he'd never felt before. He wished Hamish were here. He'd know exactly what to do, he always did.

"Och… Hamish, what will I do?" he asked aloud.

There was no need for Hamish to be there with him because Donal could hear him now. "Donal, ye ken ye must do what's right. The wee bairn needs a Da. Yer days as a randy bull must end and ye must find a lass, settle down and raise yer wee daughter."

Donal knew that was what he should do, but without his old friend to make him feel guilty, he probably wouldn't. Instead he'd focus on what needed to be done now. As a soldier, if there was a task that needed his attention, he saw to it. He might be irresponsible in the rest of his life, but he never shirked his duties. He made a mental list, find a croft of his own and find a wife, or at the very least someone to take care of Elena. It was a simple enough plan, now he had to execute it. He took another long drink of whisky and eyed the chamber that had become his when Hamish left. It was small, as was the bed and fireplace that kept him warm on cold nights. A thin wooden door separated him from the other men who shared these barracks with him. One thing was for certain, he wouldn't miss climbing over them to get out of his chamber. The more he thought about it, the more he decided that discovering he was a father was a blessing in disguise. Nothing seemed to be going right for him, but evidently someone was watching out for him. After all, he'd be spending this night and many more in a soft bed where he would surely sleep well. So, for now he'd see where things would lead him and enjoy his stay in the castle.

~

Tina was feeling lucky to have Ashley to show her the ropes. They'd been on a tour of the castle and Ashley had introduced her to the servants who'd be caring for her during her stay. She now felt she could find her way around with little trouble, which would go a long way to easing some of the anxiety she'd been feeling from the time she arrived. As they walked around the castle, they chatted and laughed like old friends. Tina felt very comfortable with Ashley and knew that if she were staying in this time, which she wasn't, their friendship would continue to blossom.

"Edna said there were more ladies here from San Francisco," Tina said.

"Two more. Sophia works in the kitchen helping Mary. And then there's Sara. You'll love her. She's so fun. She's married to Logan and she's expecting around the same time as Helene, which means any day now."

"That seems scary to me." She thought about Donal's poor wife. Being sick in this time was so dangerous. "If I ever have children, I'm planning on doing it in the hospital."

"We've got a twenty-first century doctor, Dr. Ferguson. He's from Glendaloch. He'll be arriving soon."

"Does he live in this time?"

"Uh-huh. He lives in England. He's probably on his way right now. Edna would get word to him that he was needed. She makes sure we're all okay healthwise."

"That's a nice bonus."

"It is. I was so worried about having children in this time, but so far everything's been just fine. Of course, if there's ever an emergency, Edna will whisk us back to our own time right away."

"I don't know how you do it. I can't imagine living here for the rest of my life."

"Like I told you, we're one big family. Without them I couldn't do this either." She tickled Elena under the chin and was rewarded with a giggle. "So tell me what your sister's doing."

"She's got her own band now with Hamish and my brothers." Tina felt the old pangs of jealousy that came up whenever someone was more interested in talking about Elle than anything else Tina might have to say.

"Singing the music she loves?" Ashley asked.

Tina nodded. "She's very happy. Happier than I've ever seen her."

"You'll tell her we all said hello and we're rooting for her?" Ashley tipped her head in question.

"Of course." Something she'd done seemingly a million times before and probably would do a million times more.

"I wonder who it is that Edna has in mind for you," Ashley said.

Tina was a little surprised at the change in topics. "You don't know?"

"She didn't tell us you were coming."

"Oh," Tina said, her disappointment showing.

"It's always a surprise when someone arrives from the future," Ashley assured her. "I wouldn't worry too much about figuring out who the guy is. Whoever he is, he'll be perfect for you."

Ashley's confidence helped, but Tina wasn't sure how she could be so certain. "How do you know?"

"Because Edna is an amazing matchmaker. She loves love. It's her mission in life to find people's soulmates and she's pretty darn good at it."

"I'm excited and a little nervous. What if I don't like him or he doesn't like me?"

"Love doesn't always come easy, but when it does, you'll know it and so will he."

"I'm glad you're so sure."

Elena began to whimper. "Mama."

"What's wrong little sweetness?" Tina soothed, picking her up and holding her close. She swayed a bit and patted her back, which seemed to settle Elena. She burrowed her little head into Tina's neck and played with the neckline of her dress with one hand. "My niece used to do that when she was a baby." She looked up and noticed that Ashley was eyeing her with a curious mix of wonder, curiosity and something else. From the furrowed brow and narrowed eyes, Tina didn't think it was good.

"I wonder…" Ashley began, tapping one finger on her lips.

"What?"

"I don't want to say. I don't want to put thoughts in your head that maybe shouldn't be there."

"You're not going to tell me?" Tina was confused. "Do you know who he is?"

"Not really. I'm probably just… well, let's just say, I'm not Edna."

"Whoever it is you're thinking of is someone you don't care for, isn't it?"

"Edna wouldn't match you to him." She muttered, looking down at the floor. "Don't worry. I'm sure whoever he is, he'll be everything you ever dreamed of."

"As if my curiosity wasn't piqued before… If you change your mind and decide you want to tell me who you think it is, I'm all ears," Tina said as she rocked a happier Elena back and forth in her arms.

"You're really good with her," Ashley said, obviously changing the subject.

"Thanks," Tina replied. "I feel so bad for her. She has no Mom and Donal seems stunned to be left alone with her. Her whole life changed today and now she is surrounded by strangers. She must be so confused."

Elena contentedly sucked on her fingers, her eyelids heavy with sleep. Tina sighed. She loved her little niece and nephew and she'd love Elle's baby as well, but as much as she enjoyed her role as Auntie Tina, she wanted someone to call her Mom. Hearing little Elena call her mama touched her heart in a way that brought tears to her eyes. She'd quickly blinked them away, of course. She didn't want the people she was meeting for the first time to think her an emotional mess. At home on the ranch, she was as tough as nails. No one, but no one, messed with her and she had a tendency to take that same attitude into her dating life. She had pretty high standards and a guy didn't get a second chance with her if he fell below them. Edna had her work cut out for her if she thought it would be easy to match Tina with just anyone. He was going to have to be pretty close to perfection if this was going to work.

CHAPTER 5

"If there's anything you need while you're here, just ask." Ashley said.

"You're so sweet. I can't wait to meet the other ladies from my time."

"Tonight, at dinner. They'll be excited to meet you."

"Are you sure you don't want to tell me who Edna has in mind for me?" Tina ventured. She'd always hated surprises. As a child she'd badgered her mother and father to tell her what gifts she was getting for Christmas and her birthday. When they refused, she'd sneak into their bedroom and snoop until she found what she was looking for. So not knowing who this man was, would drive her crazy and she'd probably drive Ashley crazy trying to find out. "Or do you really not know who it is?"

"I really don't know. One thing's for sure, there are a lot of single men here. The barracks are full of them. I wouldn't worry about it too much. If I know Edna, she picked the perfect man for you and you'll know it when you meet him."

She knew Ashley's reassuring smile was meant to put her at ease, but she was worried she's made a mistake. "I hope I did the right thing. I agreed to it on a whim. Elle is so happy with Hamish and I haven't had a lot of luck in the dating department, so when Edna suggested time travel, I have to admit it didn't take too much convincing on her part to get me here."

"I was surprised to find myself in the sixteenth century," Ashley laughed, "but I wouldn't change a thing."

"I know you have at least one child, right?" Tina asked.

"I have two. A boy and a girl."

"I want a family. I want my children to grow up with Elle's. You know, be around the same age." The clock was ticking. Her brother's kids were already too old to be playmates for any children Tina might have someday. If she didn't have a baby shortly after Elle, that dream was going to go down the drain.

"I know what you mean. It's great that Jenna has a little one now. It's so much fun to watch them playing together. I know they'll be as close as Jenna and I are. We're best friends, she has always been the person I could depend on to make me laugh or have my back. I could never have imagined we would get to be sisters, but we love it."

"Do you worry about your children growing up in this time? I'd be so worried about them getting sick." Tina couldn't even begin to imagine what it would be like to live without doctors and hospitals nearby.

"Edna is only a shake of my snow globe away," Ashley said, brushing her hair back behind her shoulders.

"Snow globe?" What on earth could she be talking about?

"Yeah, she gave me one for Christmas because I was worried about my baby. I was having some postpartum anxiety."

"I think I would, too." Tina chewed on her lower lip, feeling anxious at the thought of it.

"Edna told me if I ever needed help, or if *anyone* here ever needed help, I could call to her through the snow globe. And so far it works like a charm." Ashley tipped her head and threw her hands up on either side of her head with a shrug. "Go figure."

"Good to know," Tina said. Her puzzled expression drew a giggle from Ashley.

"Let's go for a walk. I've shown you around the castle, so let's go outside to the courtyard," Ashley suggested. She grabbed a plaid and wrapped it around Tina and Elena, creating a makeshift baby carrier. "There, she'll be nice and snug." She stood back, admiring her work.

"Perfect," Tina said.

~

Donal strolled through the doors of Breaghacraig with a sack of his belongings thrown over his shoulder and whistling a lively tune. His smile brightened at the sight of the new lass descending the stairs with wee Elena in her arms.

"You look happy," Tina said, reaching the bottom of the steps with Ashley at her side.

"I am," he said, winking at her. He immediately thought better of it when he noted Tina's face go from smiling to a furrowed brow and pursed lips. Apparently she didn't appreciate the wink that had melted many a heart here at Breaghacraig.

"I'm going to show Tina around the castle. Your room's at the top of the stairs," Ashley said.

"Thank ye, Lady Ashley," he said, feeling pleased with this arrangement. "I'll be seeing ye later then, lass."

Tina nodded, still frowning at him. Most of the lasses here at the castle were charmed by him 'twas true, but this one might require more work than the others. He had no doubt he'd charm her eventually, just as he had every woman he'd ever set his sights on. He bid them good day and headed upstairs to find his room. Approaching the only open door, he peeked his head inside to find Helene, Dougall's wife, just finishing up.

"Donal," she said once she noticed him standing there. She had that same stern tone she had used with him this morning. "This is to be yer room. One of the lads will bring a cradle for Elena."

"Thank ye, Helene." He knew it wasn't in his best interest to seem happy about his new room, so he hung his head, looking as sad as possible. "'Tis good of the MacKenzies to let us stay. I dinnae ken what I'd be doing if not for them."

"Dinnae think on it." He noted her voice had softened a bit so he kept his eyes down and nodded slowly, hoping he looked even sadder. "They're good to us all and they can see that ye are in need."

"I'll find a place soon," he assured her.

"There's nae hurry. Lady Irene says ye can stay as long as ye need to." She finished straightening the blankets on the bed. "If there's anything ye need for yerself or the bairn…" She sounded almost friendly.

He brushed a nonexistent tear from his cheek, noting the look of sympathy on Helene's face.

"I'll leave ye then," she said, squeezing past him into the hallway and closed the door.

The chamber was grander than any he'd had in his life. In actual fact, he'd never had a room of his own, other than the one in the barracks and compared to this, he could hardly call that a room. As a child he'd lived in a one room cottage with his Ma and Da and eight other children. He'd taken care of himself for as long as he could remember. His mother and father worked hard and had no time to raise their children, so the children raised each other. Donal fell squarely in the middle and was often forgotten in the daily hubbub of his small home.

He ran his hand reverently over the brocade bedding atop a bed larger than any he'd ever slept in. The four poster was framed by deep burgundy velvet curtains. A small table and chair were set beneath a window, the light from which lit a path across the floor to a hearth ready to hold a warming fire. It was more than he deserved and he knew it. His reverie was interrupted by a knock on the door.

"Aye," he said.

The door opened and two lads brought in the cradle. "Where would ye like it," one of them asked.

"Here, beside the bed," he answered. The reality of his new life came back to him in that instant. He was a father. Not something he'd ever thought to be and there was nothing to be done about it.

The lads closed the door behind them as they left and Donal sat on the edge of the bed, staring at the window. Could he be a good Da? He didn't know. He'd not had much of an example at home. Much of his time was spent doing chores, while his mother and father were busy tending to all of their many duties. For his mother it was caring for their wee home and farming the small plot of land that surrounded their croft. His da did odd jobs here and there, but was seldom seen before dark. As for his brothers and sisters, when they reached the age of ten, they were each sent to foster with a family that needed them. The boys to care for the cows and sheep and the girls to be maids. He'd learned early on not to get attached to anyone in his life because they always left. While Donal was alone in this world, he was never lonely. There was always some pretty lass happy to spend time with him. They would have some fun, but they ultimately wanted too much from him. He was unwilling to give away his freedom, to be saddled with one woman for the rest of his life. Now the tide had turned and he found he needed someone. Not for himself, but for wee Elena. If he could provide that much for her, perhaps he would be a good da after all.

Tina entered the great hall for the evening meal, feeling unsure of herself. She'd had a brief rest, but was eager to join the others. She hadn't had a chance to meet everyone and this would be her opportunity. Taking a deep breath she ventured into a room filled with Highland warriors, some with wives and children, some in groups of single men. One of them was meant for her, but who? The Mackenzies were all seated at a table together. Ashley waved her over and she began her long walk through the crowded tables, but before she progressed too far, someone at a table near the front of the room stood and walked towards her. It was Donal. He looked quite handsome. Why hadn't she noticed earlier?

As he approached, her heart did a little hitch in her chest.

"Would ye do me the honor of sitting with me lass?" he asked.

"I... I don't know," she glanced Ashley's way and Donal did the same.

"She's sitting with us, Donal." Ashley's tone left no room for discussion.

Tina nodded at Ashley, then turned her attention back to Donal. "Where's Elena?" she asked.

"One of the young maids is sitting with her until I return," he replied.

"Oh, good."

He bowed his head towards Ashley and then turned back to Tina. "We'll speak later, lass."

She wondered what he wanted to speak with her about and why Ashley and Jenna were looking daggers at him. A warm smile appeared on his face before he took her hand and escorted her the rest of the way to the head table.

"Thank you," she said, feeling a bit weak in the knees. A strange feeling passed through her, one she hoped didn't show on her face.

"'Twas my pleasure," he turned and walked back to his seat, where he was greeted by other men who laughed and patted him on the back. She had no idea what they were saying. As she'd learned from Hamish, when he was excited about something it was near on impossible to understand him.

"Are you okay?" Jenna asked.

"Fine, thanks."

"If you're not, it's totally understandable. I know how overwhelming it can be."

"Oh, you mean being here in this time," Tina felt like an idiot. She thought Jenna knew how Donal had affected her, "I think I might be experiencing the time travel version of jet lag."

"Totally understandable," Ashley said.

Tina glanced down the table. She'd met everyone here. Robert, Irene, Cailin, Cormac... "Where are the other women from our time?"

"Sophia is over there with Latharn." Ashley pointed to a nearby table. "Sara's not here. They must be eating at home. She's been making a real effort to learn to cook."

"Logan seems pleased with it," Cailin chimed in. "He hasn't complained much of late. What of ye? Do ye cook, Tina?"

"I can, but I don't very often. My mother likes to be in charge of the kitchen. I help out when she needs me." She gazed out over those gathered. She had a perfect view of everyone. It was loud in the great hall, but not uncomfortably so. She saw many groups talking and laughing together. When Ashley said they were one big family, she wasn't kidding.

There certainly were many unaccompanied men, but no matter where she looked, her eyes always came back to settle on Donal. He caught her looking and winked at her again. She'd always thought guys who winked were a bit cheesy, but it was kind of charming the way Donal did it. She bestowed a sweet smile on him. Tina was quite taken with his handsome appearance. He was much taller than her. His broad shoulders and solid build were something she found quite attractive. A twinge of guilt overcame her. He'd just lost his wife, but still, she wondered, *could he be the one?* If her pounding heart was any indication, he just might be.

After dinner she'd found she was completely exhausted and excused herself from the great hall. Her room was lit with candles and a fire blazed in the hearth. There was a linen gown laid out on the bed and after she managed to get herself out of the gown Edna had given her, she slipped it over her head and climbed into the bed, which was surprisingly comfortable. She hadn't expected that. She thought for sure she'd be sleeping on straw or something similar.

As she settled into the mattress, she thought back on the last couple of days. She had traveled through time! She was really here in a castle with handsome highlanders and friendly women. She fell easily asleep.

The sound of a baby crying invaded her dreamless sleep. She sat up immediately and listened. "Elena," she whispered. She continued to listen, but the crying continued. Donal mustn't know what to do. She climbed out of bed and opened her door. The passage way was dark, so she hugged the wall as she made her way towards the crying. Tina didn't have to go far. At the very next door the crying became louder. She softly opened the door and entered. The fire from the hearth lit the room. Donal was seated on the edge of the bed, rocking a cradle and pleading with the baby. "Please, wee Elena. Dinnae cry anymore."

"Donal," Tina said.

"Lass, what are ye doing here?" he asked, standing and facing her.

It was dark in the room, but the light from the hearth cast a glow that illuminated every muscle of his chest through his shirt. Her breath caught in her throat as she moved her gaze upwards to his lips. She had the urge to smooth the worried lines from his face, but that would be too bold. Elena's cries became more insistent. Tina tried to speak, but at first only the tiniest of squeaks came out. She cleared her throat. "I heard Elena crying."

"I'm sorry she disturbed yer sleep." He turned back to the cradle, his frustration showing in the defeated slope of his shoulders.

"No. It's okay. Is she alright?" Tina moved closer to place a comforting hand on his shoulder. Yes, that is what is was, she tried to convince herself.

"I dinnae ken. She willnae sleep." He scrubbed his hands through his hair before rubbing them over his face.

"Here, let me." Tina walked to the cradle and picked Elena up. "It's okay, baby. It's okay." She patted Elena's back and rocked back and forth with her. She was glad to have a job to distract her from Donal's presence while she got her heartbeat under control. Before long Elena quieted.

"Yer magical, lass," Donal whispered.

"What?" she asked, her dazed brain trying to focus on anything but Donal.

"Ye got her to stop. What magic have ye used?"

Poor clueless man. He really had no idea what to do with babies. One benefit to everyone living in the same house was that she had spent a lot of time with her niece and nephew when they were tiny. Once you learned the sway-pat-bounce rhythm all babies seemed to love, your body never forgot. "No magic. Just a little know how."

"I'm afeared I'm nae verra skilled as a Da," Donal said as he ran his hand through his hair.

"You'll get the hang of it," she said. "Is this your only child?"

"I pray so," Donal replied and then seemed to think better of his response. "Aye. She's the only one."

"I guess it's been a long time since you last saw your wife," Tina said. She wondered about her. About them.

"Aye. So long I didnae even ken she was with child."

Tina did a quick calculation in her head and came up with about a year and a half. She wondered if that was normal for men in this time. That couldn't be right. Ashley lived with her husband and there were a lot of families in the great hall at dinner. It must not have been a very happy marriage for them. "No one told you?"

"Nae. I found out today."

"No wonder you seemed so shocked." She thought *her* day had been busy.

"Why do ye think she cries so? Does she miss her Ma?" He seemed truly puzzled as he paced back and forth in front of her.

Her heart went out to him. Whatever issues their marriage had, she was gone now and he was trying to find a way forward. She tried to think of what to say that would make him feel better. "I don't know. She could be cutting teeth." The confused look on his face caused her to giggle. "Her teeth might be coming in. It can be quite painful."

"Ah," he said.

She wondered what they did for teething babies in this time. She'd ask Ashley in the morning, but for now she'd do whatever worked to calm Elena and get her to sleep. Standing here next to Donal, Tina felt at ease.

JENNAE VALE

"I'm afraid I dinnae ken how to care for a babe. Cailin and Cormac have told me I must learn."

"They're right, but it's not so hard. You can do it," she assured him.

"I'm happy ye've faith in me, but I dinnae. What do I do first?"

She regarded him and thought back to her brother's first baby. There had been so many books and blogs to read through. She thought about their shopping lists for baby items, a bunch of stuff that simply wasn't available here, but the general care of a baby probably hadn't changed that much in five hundred years. "Let's see, you'll need to learn to feed her, clothe her, bathe her…"

She looked up at him while he silently regarded Elena. Her little fists made their way into her mouth and he just looked so lost. She went to him and touched his arm.

"Don't worry. There are so many people here to help."

He looked at her hand on his arm and sighed, "I dinnae think they wish to help me," he said.

"Why not?"

"They tell me I must do it myself," he replied.

"Well, we'll see about that," she said, her take charge attitude showing. "They can't possibly mean to leave you alone to handle all of this."

"They believe they're helping me by not helping me," he explained.

"Well, it is true, the only way to learn to be a parent is to do it. But listen, I'll help you whenever I can."

"'Twould be a blessing, but I'd ask that ye nae say a word to anyone. They may nae allow it."

Tina was confused by this. She thought, from what she'd heard, that everyone here was helpful to anyone in need. She couldn't understand how they could be so mean.

Donal shifted closer to her and placed an arm around her as he looked at his daughter. For a moment, Tina wanted to lean into the strength she felt there, then caught herself and leapt away as though the very heat of him had burned her.

"I'm sorry lass. She looks so content in yer arms. I forgot myself for a moment." Donal gazed at her looking quite remorseful.

"It's okay." Tina felt all kinds of weird. Here she was alone with

Donal in his bedchamber. Realizing for the first time that she was in nothing but her linen shift. Thank goodness he was still dressed. What if someone had walked in on them? It might just ruin her chances at meeting the man of her dreams.

"Are ye sure? I didnae wish to make ye feel uncomfortable."

Uncomfortable was one way to put it, but warm and oddly drawn to him would be another. She hardly knew this man and yet she felt something passing between them that seemed like more than lending a helping hand.

"I'm sorry. I overreacted. It's not like you were trying to…"

His eyebrows scrunched together and his lips pursed as he tipped his head waiting for her to finish.

"Oh, never mind. It's fine." He was really quite good looking. Just the kind of guy she had always wished for, but could never find. Real romance novel material. Tall, strong, impossibly blue eyes paired with dark hair. She liked that.

"Are ye well, lass?"

She realized she'd been staring at him as she made a list of all his fine attributes. "Yes. Definitely. It looks like Elena has finally fallen asleep." She gently set her in her cradle. "I'll head back to my room. I'm right next door, so if you need me… I mean if Elena… If you need help, I'm right there." She finally managed to string the right words together as she made her escape out the door.

~

Donal smiled to himself as he disrobed and got into bed careful not to wake Elena. He knew the look Tina'd been giving him, he'd seen it before. Plenty of times. There was a difference here though, he felt something more for her than he had with all those other women he'd been with. He admired her ability to soothe Elena and her willingness to help him. He also admired her lovely figure, which had been quite visible in the firelight as it shone through the gauzy shift she wore. He'd been careful not to stare, but it had taken every ounce of self-restraint he possessed not to. Her soft brown locks fell in lustrous ringlets over her shoulders and down to touch the tips of her breasts. She couldn't be just another roll in the hay, she would be his salvation. He didn't have much time though. She said she was only here for a short visit. He'd have to work fast if he was to convince her to stay and mother wee Elena. If he had to be married, she'd do nicely.

CHAPTER 6

"Donal has a baby?" Sara exclaimed. "I didn't know he was married." Tina thought if her eyes opened any wider they might pop right out of her head.

"None of us did," Ashley said.

Ashley had asked Tina if she wanted to come with her to visit Sara this morning and Tina had been more than happy to join her. She thought it odd none of them knew Donal was married. From what she'd seen Breaghacraig was like a small town. Everyone knew each other and they all knew each other's business.

"Go figure," Sara said. "I guess anything's possible around here." She poured some tea for each of them and placed some oddly shaped muffins on the table.

"It's sad that she passed though, don't you think?" Tina asked, wondering at the lack of empathy she was seeing from these two women.

"Oh, of course it's sad," Sara exclaimed. "It's terribly sad. Do we know who she was?"

"No. I'm afraid not. All we know is her name was Sionaid."

"That's a pretty name," Sara said, helping herself to one of the muffins.

"Wait. I just thought of something. It wouldn't be Sionaid who worked in the kitchen, would it?" Ashley asked.

"I don't think I know her. I haven't been here as long as you have," Sara said.

"Hmmm… She hasn't been around for quite a while."

"Well, we aren't going to figure out this mystery today," Sara said. "Tina, Edna sent you to find your man. How exciting!"

Tina had just taken a bite out of one of the muffins and was unable to speak. She had been told Sara was learning to cook and she imagined that would be a doubly hard thing to do here with no modern appliances or tools. She sipped her tea to help moisten the contents of her mouth before swallowing and stifling a cough.

"They're dry. I know," Sara said. "They're better than the last batch I made. Those were as hard as rocks. Poor Logan. He always tells me they're good, no matter how bad they are."

"The tea's delicious," Tina said. She wasn't going to say anything about the muffins, but she wasn't lying about the tea. It really was good.

"Thanks. My friend, Ayla, used to live in this cottage. She gave me the recipe and showed me how to grow the herbs to make it."

"You know this would sell like crazy in our time," Tina said. "People would go nuts over it."

"Maybe I'll give you the recipe and you can give that a try," Sara suggested. "I'm not going back anytime soon."

"You really like it here?" Tina asked.

"I do, but Edna promised me that if I ever wanted to go back. I mean, if Logan and I ever wanted to go back, she'd get us there."

"It's nice that you have that option," Tina said.

"Well, I kind of forced her to send me," she shrugged and looked past Tina. "I do miss my brother, though." She absently wiped a tear from her eye and Tina felt terrible for her.

"That must be hard."

"It is, but I know I'll see him again, one way or the other. Ignore these tears! Ugh! Pregnancy hormones are in over drive, I tell you. I really am happy here."

Tina admired Sara's commitment to her husband. She couldn't imagine giving up her family to stay in this time. She continued sipping her tea and seriously considered the idea of bringing the recipe back with her. Maybe she could find out how to make the soap they all used, too. She didn't like the idea of sitting around and doing nothing when she got back home, maybe she could take up soap making or something. As Ashley and Sara continued talking, Tina's mind wandered to Donal. She hoped he was doing okay with Elena. As soon as they got back to the castle she decided she would check in on them.

"What are you thinking about Tina?" Sara asked.

"Oh, nothing much."

"Nothing much seems to have put a smile on your face."

"I was just thinking about how nice it is to be here with you both," she lied.

Apparently neither woman believed her. "Uh-huh," Ashley said, rolling her eyes towards Sara, who did the same.

"What?" Tina asked. "I mean it."

"Sure you do. Who were you really thinking about?"

"Baby Elena," she admitted. She purposely left out Donal. It was obvious from what she'd seen and heard, they weren't fans.

"She is cute, isn't she?" Ashley said.

"I'm going to have to come to the castle so I can meet her."

"Don't walk over there by yourself," Ashley said.

"I'm kind of a klutz," Sara explained. "They're all worried I'll fall or something."

"Falling wouldn't be good at this point," Tina said. "So, I agree. You should be extra careful."

"Well, I can walk back with you both then and I'll wait for Logan. Maybe we'll eat there tonight. I'm sure he'd be more than happy to have a decent meal."

"Don't sell yourself short," Ashley said. "You've been working extra hard to learn to cook. Besides, I always hear Logan bragging about you to the other men."

"Oh, he's so sweet. I just love him to pieces," Sara grinned. "So,

JENNAE VALE

Tina tell me all about Elle. What's she doing? Is she writing new songs? Is she touring?"

Tina had to admire Sara's enthusiasm. She seemed to be Elle's biggest fan, but she had kind of hoped to leave Elle in the future and make this trip all hers. "She's doing really well. She's happily married now and we just completed a European tour."

"We? Do you travel with them?" Sara asked.

"I'm the tour manager," Tina said, sounding less than happy about it.

"Oh, that sounds... um... exciting." Sara said, clearly not sure how to proceed.

Ashley seemed to understand how Tina was feeling without her even having to say a word. "It must be hard having a sister who's a celebrity. I can't even imagine what that must be like for you."

"It's never been easy," Tina said. She wasn't sure if she should reveal her deepest, darkest feelings about her sister's fame. "I never wanted to be famous," Tina said. "When Elle made it big with her first single, I was still in high school. I suddenly became very popular, but for all the wrong reasons. It wasn't me they were interested in. Guys only dated me so they could meet Elle. Everyone else only wanted tickets and backstage passes to her concerts. Don't get me wrong. I love Elle and I'm so happy for her success. It's just that now I don't know if people really like me for me or if they're just trying to get close to her. Does that make sense?"

"It does. I'm so sorry. I didn't mean to bring her up. If I'd known..."

"Don't worry about it," Tina interrupted. "It's fine. How could you possibly know about my insecurities."

"Well, I know now and I promise, from this point on my lips are sealed about your sister."

"Really, it's okay. You can talk about her all you want."

"I guess you know we won't be hitting you up for tickets," Ashley laughed.

"We like you for you," Sara assured her.

Tina smiled warmly at both women. They really were as

wonderful as she'd been told. It was nice having real friends, even if they were in the sixteenth century.

~

Donal did his best to get Elena ready for the day. He was no expert, but her dress was on and they had both survived that. He gathered her in his arms and headed for the kitchen where he hoped Mary would know what he should be feeding her. It was a boon waking up in a big, warm bed after what turned out to be a decent sleep. As he made his way through the castle, he was greeted by Irene.

"Donal, how is our wee lass this morning," she asked, chucking the bairn under her chin.

"I believe she's well," he responded. "Thank ye fer allowing us to stay."

"Yer welcome. The barracks are no place for this little one. Have ye fed her yet?"

"Nae. I'm headed to the kitchen to see what Mary has to offer."

"Take good care of her," Irene said as she walked past him into the great hall.

He wanted to tell her that it would be easier on all of them if one of the ladies of the castle took care of her, but he got the impression that they were all trying to teach him a lesson.

Entering the kitchen, Mary greeted him with a scowl and Elena with a huge grin. "So this is Sionaid's wee one, is it?"

"Aye. Mine, too, from what I've been told."

Mary swattted him on the back of the head. "Yer lucky she's the only one, the way ye spread yer seed like the farmers in spring."

He hadn't thought of that. "Do ye think there are more?" Panic began to rise from his belly to his throat and he found he'd lost his appetite.

"Aye. I do." She set a bowl of porridge down in front of him with a spoon. "For the lass."

"Her name's Elena," he said. He set the bairn on the table and she immediately reached for the porridge. He caught her before she could fall off the table or get the cooked oats everywhere. She started fussing and reaching and for such a tiny wee girl, he was having trouble holding her still. "Mary, I'm afraid I dinnae ken what to do."

"Like this." She took the spoon and put a small amount of porridge on it. Elena seemed to know exactly what to do. She stopped wiggling and fixed her eyes on the spoon, opening her mouth like a baby bird.

"Now, ye do it."

Donal did as Mary had done and was pleased Elena continued to eat. The joy he felt in this simple activity surpassed any anxiety he'd experienced only moments before.

"'Tis best she has her own spoon. Have Smithy make a wee one for her." Mary continued her work in the kitchen occasionally checking back in with him to see how Elena faired with her porridge. "Bring her back for the noon meal," she said, sounding gruff and mean to his ears.

"Mary, why do ye treat me so? If I'd known Sionaid was carrying my bairn, I would have married her." He pleaded his case to someone he'd always felt a connection to. It hurt him deeply that she was angry with him. "Please, Mary, dinnae hold it against me."

"I willnae. It will take me some time, 'tis all. Sionaid was like a daughter to me, as are all the lassies who work in the kitchen." She wiped a tear from her eye. "I'm sorry she's passed. I'm sorry for yer wee bairn, but I'm nae sorry for ye."

Her words stung him and he watched as she hurried from the kitchen as though the sight of him was more than she could bear. He wiped Elena's mouth with the cloth Mary had left on the table, feeling totally alone in the world. Perhaps rightfully so. "Come, wee one. Da has work to do." He stood and walked out into the sunshine of another day, but this day was the beginning of a new life for him. One he hadn't expected and one he wasn't sure he deserved.

As he approached the practice field, he noted that the men were already hard at work. He set Elena down on the ground where he could see her. "Ye stay right here, lass. Ye can watch yer da best the other men." He walked away, turning every so often to make sure she was still there and content to see that she was.

∼

"Oh, the men are practicing. This will be a great time for you to see which one catches your eye." Ashley winked at Tina as they approached a very large field of men in various states of undress sparring with each other. It was hard to believe men that size could move with such agility. Something caught her eye off to the side of the men.

"Is that Elena?" Tina asked.

"I think it is," Ashley said. The small tot was sitting alone on the grass some distance from the men.

Tina took off at a run, reaching Elena just as she was about to put a fist full of rocks and dirt into her mouth. She scooped her up into her arms, brushing the dirt from Elena's hands. "Where's your Da?" she asked, scanning the men in search of Donal.

"Is she alright?" Ashley asked, reaching her side along with Sara.

"She seems fine, but I can't believe Donal would just leave her here all alone."

"It's probably because he doesn't know any better," Sara said. "She's so cute." She placed Elena's hand in hers and began babbling away to her. "Who's a little cutie pie?"

"If he had any common sense, he'd know," Tina growled. "There he is." She pointed into the groups of men just as he turned to see her. Donal, being apparently none the wiser, smiled and waved to her. "He's such an idiot! She could have choked on those rocks. She could have crawled away when he wasn't looking! Grrr!"

Donal broke free from the man he was sparring with and headed towards them with a huge grin on his face.

"Are you out of your mind?" Tina shouted. "She could have been hurt! You never leave a baby alone like that!"

Donal seemed to have lost the ability to speak as he stood there, face frozen somewhere between the grin and wide-eyed shock at Tina's berating him.

"Well, don't you have anything at all to say for yourself?" she asked.

"I, I... Nae." he said, looking forlorn.

"Donal, you should have found someone to sit with her while you were out here," she scolded.

"I didnae know. I used to watch the men practice when I was a lad. I thought she would like it."

Tina put up a hand, stopping him from speaking. He didn't have baby books to read and at least he was trying, she had to remember that. "I'm sorry, Donal. I shouldn't have yelled at you. You are new at this. It's just that it scared me to think what could have happened to her. A baby her age tries to put everything in her mouth, including rocks and dirt. She could have choked, or she could crawl away before you knew she was gone. They are faster than you think." Donal went pale and Tina felt bad. Donal really was clueless. She hugged Elena closer to her chest. "I'll take her. You go back to whatever it is that you're doing. Come find us when you're through."

He reached out and touched her elbow, "Thank ye, Tina. Yer a blessing to us both." He was so close she had to crane her neck up to look into his eyes. They were the bluest she had ever seen. He bent toward her and she couldn't move. He was going to kiss her right here in front of everyone. She felt her heart nearly beat out of her chest as he placed a gentle kiss on Elena's little head and said, "Goodbye sweetling, Da will see ye later." Then he turned and headed back towards the men.

"Shall we go inside, ladies?" Ashley said.

"Lets," Sara agreed.

Tina turned to join Ashley and Sara as they headed back through the courtyard, thankful no one needed her to speak just yet.

"Remind me not to ever make you mad at me," Ashley teased.

"You were kind of ferocious with him," Sara said.

Tina was grateful for the teasing as it helped her refocus. "Only because I was afraid for Elena," she said. "I'm not usually like that." Who was she kidding? She could certainly be like that and had been on many an occasion. It was one of the reasons they made her tour manager. She had a pretty high set of standards as anyone who knew her would say, but she'd been learning that it wasn't always for the best when it came to her relationships. People had flaws. She had flaws. Accepting that about them and herself wasn't always easy for her, but she was trying.

As they entered the great hall, they were greeted by a group of children, who were introduced to her as Irene and Robert's. Sara settled herself in a chair by the hearth and motioned for Tina to do the same. "Now you get to see what Ashley does with her spare time."

A few moments later more children entered the hall and joined Ashley at one of the large dining tables set about the room. From the sounds of it, Ashley was teaching them some basic math skills. The children were all eager to learn and sat as still as could be with their full attention on Ashley.

"Does she do this every day?" Tina asked.

"Almost," Sara answered.

They spent the next hour or so listening to Ashley as she worked with the children and then finished up with a story. The children all hugged her before dashing outside to the courtyard.

"You were so good with them," Tina said.

"I used to do some teaching in my other life. I've always loved working with children."

"It's nice to have a purpose in life, isn't it," Tina said.

"It is. I'd go nuts if all I had to do was sit around doing needlework. Don't get me wrong. I like doing that kind of thing, but I love seeing the delight in the children's eyes when something finally clicks for them."

"I'm still amazed that a girl from San Francisco has managed to fit in so well in this time and place."

"Don't forget me," Sara said.

"You, too. And Jenna and Sophia, was it?" Tina tipped her head in question.

"Yes. Sophia, too," Sara answered.

"The things we do for love," Ashley said.

"Crazy, isn't it?" Sara said.

Tina silently agreed. After all, she was here in sixteenth-century Scotland looking for it. And by anyone's standards that was totally crazy. Elena had fallen asleep in her arms. She looked like a little angel as she lay there so peaceful and content, having no idea at all that life had dealt her a less than ideal hand. Tina could only hope that Donal would give her a good life.

⁓

Once done for the day, Donal went in search of Tina, knowing that Elena was safely in her care. He hadn't done much to impress Tina with his fatherly skills, but that was because he had none. He'd never been a da before, so it wasn't likely he'd be good at it. He chuckled to himself thinking about Tina. She'd thought he was going to kiss her out on the practice field. She'd closed her eyes in preparation and was surprised when it was Elena he'd kissed. She'd had that look in her eyes. The one that said she wanted him and that was a beginning. He headed towards the great hall, assuming she'd be there and he was right.

"There ye are," Donal said, as he burst into the room.

"Shhh…" Tina put a finger to her lips. "She's sleeping."

"I was thinking it might be time to feed her," he whispered.

"It probably is, but let's wait until she wakes up."

"As ye wish," he said. "Mary will have something prepared for her when she's ready."

"Speaking of which," Ashley said, "I think I'll go check on my little ones. Helene has been watching them for me. Do you want to come, Sara?"

Sara wriggled herself to the edge of the chair and Donal hurried to her side to help her up.

"Thank you, Donal. Who says you're not a gentleman?" she teased.

Donal was embarrassed by this. It hurt to know that although her tone was light, even Sara thought he was no good.

"She's only teasing you," Tina said as they both watched the ladies' departure. Was that sympathy or pity he saw in her eyes? He hoped it was neither.

"I'm nae so sure."

"I am." He rewarded Tina with a relieved smile. "Tell me more about your wife, Sionaid," she encouraged.

His smile faded. "There's nae much to tell," he said. Apparently none of the ladies told her he wasn't married. He was at odds with himself. Should he say something?

"How long were you married?" she asked.

He nervously glanced around the room as he tried not to look at Tina. Could he continue on with this ruse? This was all making him very nervous. He didn't like lying to her, but since no one had told her the truth he thought it best to stick with it. "Perhaps about two years."

"Perhaps? Don't you know for sure. When's your anniversary?" She asked, seeming surprised.

"Anniversary?" He was confused by this.

"Don't you remember the day you were married?" Her furrowed brow and wrinkled nose told him he'd better figure this out and fast.

"I do," he said. "I just don't know the exact day."

"Everyone where I come from even remembers their first date. You know, the exact time and place and they celebrate it, so remembering your wedding date is a big deal."

He was definitely in over his head in this conversation. Not knowing what to do or how to change the subject he gazed down at his feet, hoping he didn't look as guilty as he felt.

"You must have loved her very much," she said.

"Aye." She thought him sad and that would work in his favor. "We hadn't known each other long," he added. "She wished to go home and live with her parents. I stayed here. I didnae even ken she was with child. No one told me."

"That's so strange," she said and was about to continue when Elena stirred in her arms and opened her bright blue eyes. "Look who's awake." Tina glanced up at him. "She has your eyes."

"Does she?" he said, relieved that the conversation may be heading in a different direction.

"She sure does."

"I'll take her," Donal said, scooping her up into his arms. "Are ye hungry?" he asked. "Ye must be, because I am." He started towards the entry. "Are ye coming?"

"Yes," Tina said, hurrying to catch up to him.

CHAPTER 7

*D*onal couldn't believe the amount of lying he was doing to keep Tina from knowing the truth of his circumstance. He somehow knew the sympathy and compassion she'd shown him would disappear if she found out that he wasn't married to Sionaid and in fact wasn't even sure what she looked like. He'd only lain with her on one or two occasions and then he'd moved on to someone else, whom he also could not remember. His only hope was that she wouldn't find out.

They entered the kitchen and he almost immediately regretted his decision to bring Tina with him. Mary was about to open her mouth to speak, when she obviously noted Donal's pleading eyes.

"Good day to ye," she said to Tina. "I be Mary."

"Tina," she said, smiling that bright, sweet smile she had.

"Donal," Mary's tone changed. "Ye've brought the wee one back and I've made her something special." Pulling the babe from Donal's arms, Mary danced around the kitchen with her. The tinkling sound of Elena's giggle brought a warmth to Donal's heart that he had never experienced before. A deep chuckle burst from his lips as he grasped Tina's hand, giving it a small squeeze. A moment later he realized what he'd done when she pulled her hand away. "I'm sorry, lass. I was overcome with joy and I wished to share it with ye."

"It's alright," Tina said, looking anywhere but at him.

The room seemed devoid of the kitchen maid he'd been wooing this past week and for that he was grateful.

"Sit," Mary ordered. She set some food in front of them. "Eat," this command was directed at Tina who was looking through her food as if there was something hiding in it. "'Twill nae bite ye… at least I dinnae believe so," Mary laughed. "And ye, my wee lass, sit with Mary and I'll feed ye. Did ye get her spoon as I told ye?"

"Nae. I didnae have time. I will," Donal replied.

Mary's lips pressed into a narrow line as she shook her head at him.

"I will," Donal insisted. "There wasnae time this morn. I was busy."

She didn't seem convinced.

"If you tell me where to go, I'll get it for you," Tina volunteered.

"We'll go together," Donal said. "After our meal."

"Okay."

The sound of her voice was sweet to his ears as was her beauty to his eyes and her kindness to his heart. He felt content sitting here with this lass and his wee daughter.

~

Tina couldn't help feeling like part of a sweet, little family as she sat next to Donal. It was becoming more and more clear to her that he was the man she was sent here to meet. Her common sense battled with her intuition telling her she was wrong. She had to be wrong, but her intuition was winning this war. Sneaking a peek at Donal, she felt her tummy do a little flip flop and not from the food. Her assessment of his bad boy good looks, his larger than life presence and the vulnerability he showed with Elena were all very attractive to her. Never in her wildest imagination did she believe a child would come with this bargain Edna had conjured for her, but she couldn't be happier about it.

As Donal and Elena finished up their lunch, Mary tsk tsked at what was left on Tina's plate. She didn't mean to hurt anyone's feelings it was just that the food wasn't what she was used to.

"Shall we go in search of a spoon?" Donal asked.

"I'd love to," she responded.

"Ye dinnae need to search, Donal," Mary said, handing Elena back to him.

"I ken it, Mary." Donal gritted his teeth as he spoke. "I'm nae daft."

"I wouldnae be so sure," Mary said, obviously her parting shot as they walked out into the courtyard.

"She doesn't like you very much," Tina observed. She felt bad for him. He'd just lost his wife, found out he had a daughter to care for and no one seemed to have any sympathy for him. Well, she did. "I just don't understand it."

"Nor I," he said.

The sadness in his voice touched her heart and she reached out to take his hand. "I like you," she said, hoping he could hear the sincerity in her voice.

"Thank ye. 'Tis good to know."

"So, where are we going?"

"To the smithy," he replied. "to get my wee lass her verra own spoon."

They strolled through the courtyard, hand-in-hand drawing the stares of those they passed. The fact that Donal had recently lost his wife made her feel guilty and a little self-conscious. She made a conscious decision not to let it bother her. Maybe it wasn't normal for a woman to hold hands with a man in this time, but she didn't really know any of these people and she wasn't staying here. She wondered how Donal would feel about leaving. That thought hadn't occurred to her until this very moment. "Donal, do you like living here?"

"Aye. 'Tis my home."

"What if there was something you wanted in your life that wasn't here?"

"It would have to be something verra good. Something I couldnae live without. Why do ye ask?"

"Just wondering."

They arrived at the smithy, who stood over a blazing fire. "Ye should stay out here," Donal said, handing Elena into her care. "'Tis too hot in there for her."

"Okay." She watched him with a new appreciation as he spoke with the blacksmith, who it seemed had some spoons already made. Donal picked them up and examined every one until he found the spoon he must have thought to be perfect.

"I'll take this one," he said, reaching into his sporran and handing payment to the man. Donal held it up in front of his face as he came back to them. "What do ye think, Elena? Will this one do?"

She held out her hand and was rewarded with her very own spoon. She waved it around before promptly dropping it. Donal retrieved it with a grin and placed it in his sporran. They walked around the courtyard together for a while longer enjoying the warmth of the sun and each other's company.

"'Tis been a good day," Donal noted.

Tina was pleased to hear this because she was thinking the exact same thing. "The next thing we need to find for you is someone to look after Elena while you're working."

"Aye. Yer right. 'Twouldnae be fair to ask ye to spend all yer days here looking after her."

"Don't get me wrong. I don't mind helping. As a matter of fact, I really enjoy it, but I'm going to need back up."

He was looking at her with a confused expression.

"I'm going to need help," she explained.

"Where will we find someone?" he asked.

"Let me see what I can do. I might have better luck with it than you." The way everyone was treating him she had no doubt they'd probably run the other way if he were to ask.

"Ye'd do that for us?" he asked. The poor guy couldn't believe someone was willing to help him.

"I already told you I'd help in any way I can."

"So ye have," he smiled warmly at her and her belly sang with the beating of a million butterfly wings. His eyes held hers for what should have been an uncomfortably long time, but to her seemed not long enough. She thought he might kiss her when they were interrupted.

"Excuse me, miss. Ye dropped this." A girl of not more than fourteen stood before her holding up one of her earrings. She instinctively checked both ears and realized that one of her earrings had fallen out.

"Oh, thank you. I wouldn't have noticed until much later and by then probably wouldn't have had a chance of finding it."

"Yer welcome, miss." The girl's eyes were glued to little Elena. "How old's yer bairn?"

"Oh, she's not mine. She belongs to Donal and she's… ten months old." That seemed about right. "What's your name?"

"Doreen," the girl said, tickling Elena's toes and making her laugh. "She's verra sweet."

"She is, isn't she?" Tina said. An idea was beginning to form. "Do you like babies, Doreen?"

"I do, verra much. Some day I hope to have a house full of them, like me ma."

"So you have lots of brothers and sisters?" Tina asked.

"Too many to count," Doreen laughed. "I'm the oldest, so I help ma with the little ones when she needs me to," Doreen said, seeming proud of herself.

"Doreen, how would you feel about watching Elena every now and again?" Tina asked, crossing her fingers that she would.

"I'd love to," the girl answered.

"Could you start tomorrow? Donal would be happy to pay you for your services." This was going to be the medieval version of babysitting.

"Do ye ken how to do it?" Donal asked, sounding concerned as any good Da should.

"Aye. Ye've nae need to worry. I've done it before."

"Meet me here tomorrow morning then," he said, seeming more relaxed.

The girl beamed with joy as she thanked them and spun away to join her friends, excitedly telling them what had just occurred.

JENNAE VALE

"There, problem solved," Tina said. "She can't watch her all the time, so when she's not able, I will."

"Thank ye, lass. Me heart will rest easy now."

"You should probably take her upstairs. She probably needs some sleep."

They entered the castle and Donal left her to go up to his room. She entered the great hall where Ashley had just finished up with the afternoon lessons. Children scurried past Tina and out the door. "All done for the day?" she asked.

"I am. What have you been up to all day?" Ashley asked.

"I think I figured out who Edna had in mind for me," she said.

"Tell me! I can't wait to hear." Ashley seemed quite excited at her news.

"I think it's Donal," Tina said and watched as Ashley's face dropped.

"No. It can't be," she said.

"Why not?" Tina was feeling a bit defensive. "What's wrong with Donal?"

"Oh, nothing. I just didn't think he'd be the one. You know with the baby and all. It doesn't seem like Edna would send you here to find a man who already has a family."

Tina watched as Ashley danced around her initial reaction. No matter what she said now, Tina knew she wouldn't be an ally as far as Donal was concerned.

"You should still just see if anyone else catches your eye. You might be wrong. You never know."

"You're right," Tina said, knowing that she wasn't, but not wanting to be judged. "I should keep my options open."

"That's probably the best idea," Ashley said. "I'm going to enlist Cailin's help. He knows all the men who would be eligible bachelors."

"Thanks," Tina said, filling her voice with feigned enthusiasm. What was wrong with Donal? Was there something she was missing?

Donal wasn't surprised at the light tap on his door. Although he'd tried his best to quiet her, Elena's continued crying was sure to wake Tina. He should feel bad about that but he had to admit he was glad to see her.

"Come in," he said.

"Is she alright?" Tina asked, going immediately to the cradle.

"I've been rocking her, but she still cries." How was a person to know what babies wanted when they just cry and cry? Every time she stirred he'd sat up and gently rocked the cradle. That had worked through most of the night, but now she was just crying for no reason and the rocking wasn't working.

"Oh, you poor baby." She reached into the cradle and rubbed Elena's belly before lifting her into her arms. "Do you mind if I sit?" Tina asked.

He patted the edge of the bed to let her know he didn't mind. He'd propped himself on one elbow and made sure he was covered from the waist down. Tina rubbed Elena's back and gently rocked back and forth. In no time, Elena was snuggled into her neck and yawning, she was still fussing but the crying had stopped. So rocking did work, he was the one doing it wrong. Although truth be told, he was quite sure that if he was allowed to snuggle into Tina's neck, he would find peace there, too.

"You must be tired," Tina said.

Donal stifled a yawn. "Nae. I be fine."

She shook her head at him and rolled her eyes. "You don't have to be the big, strong man around me, you know."

She thought him big and strong, which pleased him. Tina placed Elena on the bed and continued to rub her belly. "I think she's got a tummy ache."

That made him sit up completely alert. "What can be done?" He hadn't even considered that the bairn could be in pain.

"I don't know, but this seems to be helping."

There was magic in those hands, he thought. Elena's fussing, turned to whimpers and then disappeared altogether as she closed her eyes and drifted off to sleep. Tina continued gently rubbing and Donal lay back in the bed feeling the weight of the world had been lifted from his shoulders by a wee lass from the future. He closed his eyes and felt the bed shift as Tina lay across the foot of the bed. His lips curved upward. Somehow she had taken all his worries from him, leaving him in a more peaceful place. What would he do when she left him… left them? It was something he didn't wish to think about, so instead he pretended she was staying and saw himself in a small cottage with her at his side and his wee daughter playing at their feet. It was a pleasant thought and one he was determined to make come true.

Morning broke and Tina awoke to find herself back in her own bed. She didn't remember falling asleep and she didn't remember returning to her room. Donal must have carried her there. Her foggy memory suddenly cleared. He had. She could feel his strong arms as they lifted her from the bed. Her head had rested in the crook of his neck where she burrowed in. She heard the sound of a very manly groan close to her ear and felt a gentle kiss on her forehead as the blanket was lifted to cover her. "Goodnight to ye, lass," he'd said before leaving her. She was happy she hadn't forgotten and the memory of it aroused her in ways she hadn't felt in ages. Ashley had to be wrong. He was the one. Why else would she wake longing to see him?

She hurried from her bed and ran downstairs to the great hall expecting to find him there, but instead she found Doreen playing with Elena. "Good morn to ye, miss."

"Good morning, Doreen. How's Elena this morning?" She felt Elena's forehead and was rewarded with a smile. "She seems quite happy this morning."

"Aye. She seems well."

"She's been having trouble sleeping," Tina explained.

"I'll see to it that she gets a rest later this morn."

"Good. Where did Donal go?" She hoped the breathiness of her voice didn't belie her interest.

"I dinnae ken. He said he'd be back later."

"Hmmm..."

"Is something wrong?"

"No, Doreen. I thought I'd have breakfast with him."

"He's been gone for some time." If she said she wasn't disappointed, she'd be lying to herself. She'd been looking forward to seeing him and had rushed downstairs with that thought in mind.

"Come sit and have breakfast with us," Jenna said as she entered the hall. "Ashley will be right down."

"Alright." She followed Jenna to the table and sat next to her.

"I see Donal found a babysitter for Elena," Jenna observed, nodding towards Doreen.

"Yes. She seems quite capable."

"She is. She's helped me and Ashley on more than one occasion."

"Poor Donal really needed the help," Tina said.

"I don't doubt it. He's not the most responsible man around," Jenna said, rolling her eyes skyward.

"What is that supposed to mean?" Tina was irritated for Donal. He seemed quite responsible to her.

Before Jenna could answer, Ashley joined them. "I talked to Cailin last night and he has a few prospects for you."

"Are we matchmaking?" Jenna asked.

"We are."

"I'm curious to know who he picked. I've been talking with Cormac about the same thing. It'll be interesting to see if they've come up with the same names."

Tina wasn't sure this was how it was supposed to work. "Isn't Edna the matchmaker?"

"She is, but a little help from us wouldn't hurt. Besides, if you don't like them, you can tell us. We won't mind."

Tina carefully schooled her reaction. "Alright." She didn't care who they picked for her. She knew what she wanted and Donal was it. She only hoped he felt the same way.

"So, who did he pick. Names, please." Jenna leaned her elbow on the table and peered past Tina to see Ashley.

"Tam, Jock and Marcas," Ashley beamed.

"They were Cormac's choices, too."

"And good ones," Ashley said, glancing at Tina.

"Don't worry about a thing, Tina. We'll arrange everything. You'll get to spend some time with each of them and then you can make your choice."

I've already made my choice, she thought. "I think I need some fresh air. I'll talk to you later," Tina said, rising to leave.

"Is everything okay?" Ashley asked.

"Fine," she replied. How could she tell them this wasn't what she wanted? They were just trying to be helpful.

"We'll start working on this for you," Jenna called after her.

She couldn't walk out of the hall fast enough and was relieved when she reached the doors to the courtyard. If only Elle were here. She'd understand.

She descended the steps and headed for the gate. She needed to get away so she could think.

"Tina!"

She turned to see Donal hurrying towards her with a small bouquet of wildflowers in his hand. Her heart thudded in her chest at the sight of him and the closer he got, the louder it thundered in her ears.

"These are for ye," he said, handing them to her.

"Thank you," she lifted them to her nose and their sweet scent calmed her. "They're beautiful."

"As beautiful as ye," he replied.

She felt the heat of his gaze as a flush of warmth penetrated her from head to toe. "And thank you for carrying me back to my room last night."

"I would have left ye there. Ye looked so peaceful laying next to Elena, but I didnae wish to soil yer reputation."

"That's very thoughtful of you." How could anyone think poorly of him? He was a good man and she was a good judge of character. One thing she prided herself on was her ability to read people.

"Doreen is with Elena. She seems to be in good spirits this morning, thanks to ye."

He looked away and shifted his weight. Looking first towards the gate and then back at the castle. There was uncertainty in the movement and Tina realized he was nervous.

"I was thinking… that is… I wondered if ye'd like to walk with me to the village."

Tina felt her smile spread across her face and down to her toes. "I'd love to," she said.

"You would?" He seemed surprised, but caught himself and said, "It is nae too far and the weather is quite fine." He took her hand and tucked it under his arm, smiling down at her with the most beautiful smile. She stared at his lips for a moment before raising her eyes to meet his. She saw there what she imagined was the same thing she was feeling. She licked her lips and gazed at the dirt path in front of them.

They passed others as they walked and Donal nodded a greeting to them. Tina felt she was in a bubble that muted the sights and sounds around her, leaving her fully aware of the man beside her. With every brush of his arm on hers, a tingle of excitement passed through her.

CHAPTER 8

"Are ye hungry?" Donal asked. They'd been walking for a while now. He'd shown her around the village where he'd purchased a small doll for Elena and some ribbons for Tina's hair. She'd protested, but he could see she was touched by his gesture.

"I am," she replied.

He took her hand and led her into the village inn. Finding an empty table in a back corner, he pulled out a chair for Tina and then sat next to her.

"I've really had a nice day. Thank you, Donal."

"'Tis been a pleasure to be at yer side." A bit of pink tinged Tina's cheeks. "I'm sorry. I've embarrassed ye."

"You've been so sweet to me today. I can't remember the last time someone thought it was a pleasure to be with me."

"I don't believe it. A lass as lovely as yerself? Ye must have many men vying for yer attentions."

"I don't," she replied, and when his expression told her he didn't believe her, "Really."

"The men where yer from must all be daft then." That earned him a smile and he felt ten feet tall.

"Donal, we haven't seen ye of late," Tess said as she approached the table. "Where have ye been?"

Donal wanted to shrink into nothing. Tess had been one of his many conquests. He hadn't thought of that when he'd chosen to bring Tina here. Perhaps this wasn't such a good idea. It seemed no matter where he went he ran into someone who knew all his secrets. He was going to have to get better at not revealing them. He hoped Tess would keep her mouth shut. "I've been busy," he heard the gruffness in his voice, but there was naught to do about that.

"He's usually here most nights," she said to Tina, who didn't reply.

"Well, I won't be from now on. I've other things to occupy my time," Donal stated.

"This one?" she said, nodding towards Tina. "She looks to be too good for ye." Tina was staring at the table, avoiding him and Tess, pretending she couldn't hear a word they were saying. Just when he was making progress. He had even picked flowers for her. Tess was going to wreck everything, he had to get rid of her.

"We'd like some food if ye dinnae mind," he said.

"Of course," she said, turning to walk away.

"And ale," he called after her. "I'm sorry about that," he said to Tina.

"Why?" she asked.

"She's a bit troublesome, if ye ken my meaning." With any luck, he could keep Tess from ruining the rest of his day with Tina.

"She was trying to make you look bad," she said.

"Aye. That's it. She was." Luckily Tina didn't know him well enough to understand that she wasn't trying to make him look bad. He simply was bad. He'd brought many a lass to this very tavern and now he'd brought Tina to this place where everyone knew him and knew his womanizing ways. Why hadn't he thought of that? It would have been better to take her back to Breaghacraig instead.

"Maybe she thinks it odd that you're spending time with me so soon after your wife passed." She reached for his arm with a comforting touch.

"That could be it." He was going to have to tell her the truth sooner or later, but she was looking at him with such sympathy in her eyes that he thought much later would be best. "Yer beauty is only surpassed by yer kindness," he said, wishing to see if he could pinken those cheeks once again.

Her eyes misted over as she looked down at her hands. He had touched her heart. He could see it. The strange thing was that he found he truly meant it. He'd never met a lass like her and doubted he ever would again. He'd never taken much time to get to know them, except for what would get them into his bed.

Tina could be so strong and sure, like when she yelled at him during practice yesterday. But now she seemed so delicate, like the wildflowers that were wilting in her pocket. He wanted to know everything about her.

Tess brought their food and ale. Tina once again poked through it before deciding to eat. The ale didn't seem to be to her liking either, so Donal drank it. As they ate, his leg brushed up against hers beneath the table. He was pleased when she didn't move it away, but he was surprised by his own reaction. Every nerve ending tingled with those brief touches as both his pulse and desire quickened. Tina was different. He had to take his time with her. She wasn't just a quick roll in the hay. This would take patience on his part. He tamped down the desire that was causing him to shift uncomfortably in his seat and cleared his throat. "We should get back. Doreen will wonder where I've been." He got to his feet and held out his hand to Tina, who took it as she rose. He was in uncharted territory with this lass. He only hoped he was up to the challenge.

∼

As they approached the castle, Tina saw Ashley, Cailin, Jenna and Cormac standing together with another man she hadn't met.

"Tina," Ashley called to her.

"I'm sorry. I should go see what she wants. Thank you again for a fun day."

"Yer welcome, lass. We'll do it again soon." Donal took her hand and placed a lingering kiss upon it.

Her legs felt weak beneath her. No one had ever kissed her hand before. She liked it. She watched as Donal walked away, enjoying the sight of his strong back and legs as he made his way to the castle doors.

"Tina," Ashley called again.

"I'm coming," Tina hurried over to the group. "Sorry about that."

"I wanted to introduce you to someone. Tina, this is, Tam."

"I'm enchanted to meet ye," he said with a bow of his head.

"It's nice to meet you, too," she answered. Darned if they hadn't gone ahead with their matchmaking scheme. She should have shut them down this morning, but she hadn't. Now, she didn't feel she had much choice but to go along with it. They were her hosts after all. It would probably be a good thing. A chance to confirm that she had made the right choice. Yes, that was it. She wouldn't feel anything for this man and then she'd know for sure that Donal was the man for her.

"Tam is one of me best men," Cailin said, glancing from one to the other. "He'll be joining us for the evening meal."

"That's nice," Tina said. This had to rank right up there as one of the most incredibly awkward moments of her life. She really wanted to bolt, but that wouldn't have been very polite. She'd behave and stay put, no matter how much her feet insisted that she run away.

"How are you enjoying your stay at Breaghacraig?" Tam asked.

Well, she had been having a lovely day with a different man until now. She couldn't say that. She didn't really know what to say since most of her time had been spent with Donal and Elena. She wondered how Elena was doing this afternoon, and whether her tummy ache had returned. She looked around and realized she hadn't answered his very polite question. To make matters worse, Tam hadn't taken his eyes off of her and she couldn't seem to look at him. She needed to say something. Maybe that would help. Having a conversation would make things less awkward.

"It's a beautiful day." She couldn't believe she'd come all the way to the year 1518 to discuss the weather, but that's exactly what she was doing.

Tam chuckled. "I believe we've made ye wish ye were elsewhere."

A relieved laugh escaped Tina's lips. "No. Not at all."

"There's nae need to spare my feelings," he teased.

Okay. Maybe this wouldn't be so bad. He seemed nice enough and he understood she wasn't on board all the way with this matchmaking. She glanced around and noticed that while she'd been busy looking down at the ground, the others had all snuck away. "I think I'm going to go rest. It's been a busy day for me and the last thing I want to do is fall asleep while I'm eating." She was babbling and Tam seemed to get it.

"Until tonight," he bowed to her slightly before turning and walking away.

Closing her eyes, she shook her head and let out a big breath. *You can do this, Tina. You can do this.*

Donal entered the great hall, hoping to convince Tina to sit with him, but much to his dismay he saw that she was already seated with Tam who had been invited to sit with the Mackenzies. Tina was laughing at something he'd said and he placed an arm around the back of her chair as he gazed into her face. Donal felt his blood boiling. They had spent half the day together, and half the night, too. Why was she with Tam? He felt betrayed by his friend, by the Mackenzies, and by Tina. Was no one on his side? He thought he'd made progress today. Thought she would be the woman for him. The one who would save him from himself and care for his daughter. His plans were truly ruined, but there was something else. A new emotion he'd never felt before. Could he be jealous? He'd never cared enough about the women he'd known to feel it and he wasn't sure that was what it was. It welled up in him from the pit of his stomach, invading his brain and knocking any good sense he had out of the way. He clenched his fists and stalked to a table occupied by his friends. How was he to sit here and watch this? In his mind Tina was already his. He was going to have to have a little talk with Tam.

"Yer looking quite angry," Jock said as Donal plunked himself down on the bench next to him.

"Aye."

"Did the kitchen maid turn ye down again?" Marcas asked, turning to laugh with the other men.

It was the wrong question and it was all Donal needed to lunge at his friend, grabbing him by the throat and lifting him to his feet. "Watch what ye say!" he growled, tossing him backwards onto the floor.

The room grew silent around them. Donal realized he'd made a mistake when he glanced up to see Tina with a look of horror on her face, her hand covering her mouth. Marcas wanted to retaliate and struggled to get to his feet, but was restrained by the others around him. With one last angry look at the Mackenzie table, he strode from the hall and out into the courtyard. It wasn't often that Donal lost his temper. Until a couple of days ago, he was a very relaxed kind of guy, friendly with everyone and quick with a joke. But his life was a mess and just when he thought he was getting it back on track, he attacked a friend. This had to have been the worst time for him to do so. Tina would never look at him the same way again. He'd ruined everything. Not knowing what to do or where to go, Donal stood motionless, arms at his side, head and shoulders slumped in shame and defeat.

"Donal!" Logan's voice called to him from the castle doors.

He didn't move and didn't respond. He could hear Logan striding up behind him and was ready for whatever might come his way.

"Donal, what was that all about?" Logan asked. There was no judgement or anger in his voice.

"I dinnae know," Donal responded.

"It's not like ye to do something like that."

"My apologies," he muttered, unable to face Logan.

"I'm nae the one ye need to apologize to. Tell me what Marcas has done."

Donal sighed and turned to his friend. "There was nae need for my behavior. I was angry when I sat down and something Marcas said…"

Logan put an arm around his shoulders and got him to walk away from the castle. "So if it wasnae Marcas ye were angry with, then who or what?"

"Ye ken how yer always telling me I need a wife?"

"Aye."

"I never believed it, but now there's Elena. And she needs a Ma…"

"So this is about Elena?"

Donal searched his heart. Elena needed a mother, but he needed Tina more. More than someone to care for the bairn, she was someone that made him want to be better than he was. "Not really. I believed I'd found the woman I wanted, someone that I wanted in my life, but she was seated with someone else."

"So ye were jealous?"

Is that what the tight feeling in his chest was? "I've never felt this way before. Never had cause to be jealous."

"Then it must be love."

Logan was not making this easier for him. First jealousy and now love? He had never been more confused in his life. "I dinnae ken if 'tis, but I feel things when I'm with her that I've nae felt before."

"May I ask who it is?"

"Tina. The lass from the future."

"Well, that makes sense then," Logan mused. "Sara told me that Ashley and Jenna were looking for the right man for her. I believe ye think yer the one."

"I thought so, but now after what just happened." He turned and caught Logan's eye, then shook his head in shame. "I saw the look on her face. She'll nae want me now."

"You don't know that. You should talk to her," Logan suggested.

"She's with Tam tonight."

"That shouldnae stop ye. Explain what happened. As Sara always tells me, ye need to use yer words." He chuckled at this.

"Use yer words?"

"Instead of yer fists."

Donal nodded his understanding. "That would have been useful to know before I tried to kill Marcas," he chuckled. "Yer wife is verra wise."

"She is," Logan beamed. "'Tis one of the many reasons I love her so."

Despite all of his faults and inadequacies, Donal knew that Logan was on his side. He'd been feeling of late that anyone who knew him thought him unworthy. Perhaps they thought he'd finally gotten what he deserved. In some ways maybe he had. It hurt that Lady Ashley and Jenna were trying to find a man for Tina. But if he was being honest, he might do the same thing in their position. Why would they want someone as kind and generous as Tina to be with someone so careless as to not even remember the names of women he had known. He was sure he couldn't feel any lower than he felt at this moment, but he was more determined than ever to prove them wrong. He wasn't that thoughtless man any more. He was trying hard to change. He could be a good da to Elena. He could be as good a man as any who resided at Breaghacraig and he could be the kind of man who was worthy of Tina's love.

"Thank ye, Logan."

"Will ye come back in and join us?"

"Nae. 'Tis best that I punish myself by eating in the kitchen with Mary." In fact, he was far too embarrassed to go back in to the stares of those in the hall.

Logan burst into laughter. "She'll be sure to set ye straight. I'm here to listen if ye choose to use yer words."

"I may take ye up on that offer."

Logan walked back into the great hall and Donal banished himself to the kitchen where, true to form, Mary showed him no sympathy.

"What happened?" Tina asked no one in particular as she watched an angry Donal storm from the hall.

"Someone let their temper get the better of them," Ashley said.

What she'd just witnessed had been downright scary. The man Donal had attacked was being held down by three other large Highlanders. She hoped he didn't go after Donal once they let him go.

"Dinnae fear, lass. Logan has gone after Donal to see what's got him so riled," Cailin assured her.

Deep in her heart she thought she knew exactly what it had been. She'd seen him enter the hall out of the corner of her eye and his expression went from happy to angry in a flash when he saw her sitting with Tam.

"Is this normal around here?" she asked.

"I wouldn't say it's normal, but it's definitely not something you should worry about. They usually work things out when they're sparring with each other."

"I've never seen anyone get that angry." She was sure she didn't want to see it again. She knew many of the men here were warriors. She had seen them training and sparring. It hadn't really occurred to her how that training would play out when they were angry. She'd only known Donal for a short time, maybe he had a bad temper. She wasn't sure she could live with that. Tina was rethinking the whole Donal-is-the-one thing.

"Come sit, lass." Tam guided her back to her seat.

"Thank you, Tam." He really was being a gentleman tonight. Of course, he might have a dark side, too. She had seen him on the practice field wielding a sword with the others. "I think Donal was angry that I was sitting with you. I hope he doesn't go after you."

"If he does, I'm capable of caring for myself," he smiled at her. Did he not realize how serious this was? He seemed to pick up on her discomfort and explained, "Donal is a friend. If he doesnae like it, he'll tell me." He gazed into her eyes. "What of ye? If ye'd rather be with Donal, I'll understand."

"No. I mean… I don't know. I'm confused right now." Tina looked towards the door Donal had walked out. There was so much she didn't understand about this time.

"I'll give ye all the time ye need."

"I appreciate that."

～

Tina was relieved that she didn't hear Elena crying that night. It meant that she didn't see Donal, which was probably for the best. She had some thinking to do. They'd had such a nice day together and she'd thought him to be such a gentleman with her. He spoiled it all when he decided to lose it in the great hall. She wondered if it had really been jealousy that had caused him to lose his temper. If it wasn't, she wanted to know what had been said to set him off. It was surprising how much it had frightened her. Fighting wasn't something she saw too often. Her brothers occasionally got each other in a headlock, but it never escalated to the point where she feared they might do physical harm to each other.

For as long as she could remember it had really bothered her when people around her were angry. Despite her take charge attitude and general snarkiness, it was clear to her that she put a wall up to keep people at arms length, far enough away that they couldn't possibly be angry with her, or if they were they didn't dare tell her. Tina wasn't sure where this all came from. Her family certainly weren't the type to yell and scream at each other. She'd become somewhat of a people pleaser to avoid being yelled at in school, at work or just out and about in the world. The more she thought about it, the more she realized that she was also frightened of her own anger. She hated to lose her temper, feeling that it made her look a little nuts. So she carefully kept it all in check. She certainly let people know when they disappointed her or when she thought they were wrong, but she kept all her anger locked up inside, never allowing it to see the light of day. Giving people the silent treatment and that look she had perfected, the one that said don't mess with me, was how she chose to handle most disagreeable things.

The sun peeking in through the lone window in her chamber told her it was time to get up. Unsure of what the day would hold in store for her, Tina reluctantly rose and got dressed. Had she made a mistake coming here? If she had, it was too late now to do anything about it. She splashed some cold water on her face, brushed her teeth with the odd mixture Ashley had given her and then carefully laced the dress Jenna had let her borrow. She donned the same slippers Edna had given her and, taking a deep breath, walked out of her room. It was another day to shine, as her mother always said.

CHAPTER 9

All seemed back to normal this morning at Breaghacraig. Doreen was with Elena again and Donal was nowhere to be seen. As for Tina, it seemed she'd be spending the day with Jock and Marcas. Walking out into the courtyard, she was greeted by bright sunlight and two mountainous men.

"Lady Tina," Jock approached with an outstretched hand.

"Please call me Tina. No lady required." Her nervous laughter gave away her trepidation about this outing.

"I be Jock and this be Marcas."

"Good day to ye," Marcas said.

This was the man Donal had gone after last night. She glanced around to make sure Donal wasn't anywhere nearby. The last thing she wanted or needed was for another brawl to take place over her. Some women might enjoy having two men fight over her, but Tina wasn't one of them.

"Mary has kindly packed a basket for us. We thought ye might like to sit by the water with us," Marcas said.

Tina wasn't so sure that was what she would like at all, but she had agreed to meet the other single men that Ashley and Jenna suggested so she would go through with it. "I'd love that."

She found herself sandwiched between the two men as they walked out through a side gate and along a path that sat above a strip of beach she hadn't known existed before this moment. She'd known they were close to the water, but since she'd arrived, she hadn't really had time to explore. "It's beautiful," she said. The cry of the gulls and the scent of the salt water brought her back to childhood trips to the beach with her family. She immediately relaxed. As they approached a narrow path leading down to the water, Marcas went first, holding her hand and leading her down. Jock followed behind, she imagined to catch her if she fell. Two sweet men she should consider and give a chance, as she would with Tam.

Jock spread a tartan on the beach where they sat and talked for hours. Each man took a turn to tell her about his childhood and his life here at Breaghacraig. She had so many questions for them. Where were they from? How many brothers and sisters did they have? Would they miss them if they had to move far away? That one was important to her. She wasn't planning to stay, but she didn't want to drag any of them kicking and screaming into the twenty-first century.

It occurred to her that she hadn't actually asked Donal these questions either. She thought back over the time that they had spent together and realized they hadn't shared much about their families. How could she possibly be thinking that he was the "one" when she didn't even know if he had siblings?

Marcas had some reservations about leaving his very large family to move away and couldn't see anything ever happening that would make him change his mind. Jock on the other hand seemed open to adventure, which life with her would surely be.

"So, you'd be alright moving far away from your family?"

"I would. I dinnae see them verra often. This has been my home and these people have been my family since early on."

Jock was tall, but weren't they all, with dark blond hair and hazel eyes. His features were perfect, but maybe a little too perfect. No. She was just being picky she told herself. He was strong and masculine, but he also had a gentle nature. She had no idea how she knew it, but she did. He'd make a good husband and father.

Marcas was darker in coloring, having dark brown hair and very dark brown eyes. He reminded her of her brothers. He'd fit in well with her family, but he wasn't interested in leaving his behind. That was a deal breaker for her, and she was glad to have at least one of the men off her list. There was something she wanted to ask him, but had avoided until this point. No harm in asking now, though.

"Marcas, why did Donal attack you last night?" she asked, hoping against hope that there'd been some reason for what she'd seen.

He laughed at that, "Och! I teased him about the kitchen maid. He took exception to it."

"The kitchen maid?" she asked, unsure what the kitchen maid had to with anything.

"Aye. I asked him why he was angry. Was it because the kitchen maid…" he looked down at the sand he was sifting through his fingers as he spoke. It was clear he wasn't sure if he should tell her what he wasn't saying.

"Please, you can tell me," she said, encouraging him. She had to know what had been said and why Donal reacted the way he did.

"Well, Donal has eyes for the kitchen maid, or at least he did until ye arrived. Before ye came to Breaghacraig something always got in the way of…"

This was like pulling teeth. He kept stopping right before the part she was interested in. "It's alright. You don't need to tell me." Maybe she didn't want to know. It sounded very much like Donal was planning to cheat on his wife with the kitchen maid and that made her skin crawl. He had said that they hadn't been together for months and clearly, there were a lot of issues with their marriage. But still, she wanted to believe that she would choose a partner that would never cheat. No relationship was perfect, she understood that and had seen her parents fight and make up over the years. She wanted someone that would work with her through their problems. That didn't mean Donal was the right choice, she'd seen his temper and it had frightened her. It was not something she thought she could live with.

Marcas seemed relieved as he glanced over at Jock.

"He's had some bad luck of late," Jock said. "Finding himself with a wee bairn to raise on his own would be daunting for him. When ye arrived, he thought his problems solved. He said he'd marry ye and ye'd raise the child."

"What?" Did Jock really just say that?

The men looked at each other and some sort of silent conversation was happening between them. "I'm sorry. I thought ye'd ken it. I thought he'd spoken with ye."

"No. I didn't know." So all this time, Donal had only been nice to her because he needed a wife to care for Elena. The nerve of him. She could feel the anger building inside her, but right alongside of it was a different sort of pain, one that centered near her heart. She chose to ignore that. It seemed he was just like every other guy she'd ever dated. They never just wanted her. There was always an ulterior motive where she was concerned. All they cared about was what she could do for them.

"I was surprised when Cailin asked if we'd like to… get to know ye. We both thought ye were Donal's lass."

How was she supposed to find the mystery man that Edna intended if Donal had already told them all to back off? "No. I'm not Donal's lass. I'm not anybody's lass."

She could see now she'd made a terrible mistake. She wanted to go home. Back to her own time where women weren't treated like possessions.

"I'm sorry. It seems I've upset ye."

Taking a deep breath, she calmed herself. She wouldn't let them see how bothered she was. "No. Not at all. It's good to know what his intentions were." This wasn't sitting well with her and she needed to talk to Ashley about contacting Edna. "I think I'd like to go back now, if you don't mind."

The men rose and helped her to her feet, folded the plaid and refilled the basket. As they walked back to Breaghacraig, Tina was quiet, reflecting on her expectations of this trek back in time and the reality of it. When she really thought about it, everyone had been so nice to her. Everything had seemed to be going well until this point. It was clear to her that everything wrong with this trip was due to

Donal and her expectations of him. Really it wasn't his fault. He was just being Donal and she shouldn't have expected him to meet some unrealistic vision she had of the perfect man. Obviously she hadn't found *that* man yet and it was becoming clear to her that he may not be here at all.

∼

The kitchen was as hot as it had been on her first visit, but Mary and the other women working there didn't seem fazed by it. The hustle and bustle was constant when there were so many mouths to feed.

"Good day to ye, lass," Mary said as she entered. "What can we do for ye?"

"I wondered if I might get some tea," she said. That wasn't really her reason for visiting, but she thought she'd ease into that.

"Sit right there, dear," Mary said, motioning to the table where she was busy chopping vegetables and where Sophia was kneading dough. Two other young women were also working feverishly in the background.

"Sophia? Right?" she said. "We met the other day."

"Yes. How are you?"

"Okay."

"You don't sound okay." she said.

"I'm sure you know how I'm feeling."

"Like a fish out of water?"

"Something like that."

"Here ye go, lass. Honey?" Mary asked, placing her tea down in front of her.

"Yes, please."

Mary set a small jar down for her.

"Thank you. You must be getting ready for tonight's meal," Tina said.

"Oh, aye. We're always getting ready for one meal or another." Mary set a slice of warm bread down in front of her.

"Mmmm... That looks and smells wonderful."

"Enjoy it, lass. I hear ye havenae been eating much."

"How do you know that?"

"I've heard from the lads. Jock and Marcas told me ye hardly touched the food I packed for them. And Donal says ye havenae liked the food."

Thankfully, Mary seemed more concerned than angry. Tina didn't want to offend her cooking, especially when she worked so hard to feed so many people day in and day out. "It's not that I don't like it. It's just different."

"Well, eat that bread," Mary ordered. "I dinnae wish ye to go back to yer home looking as if we didnae feed ye."

"Don't worry about that. I'm a picky eater at home, too."

Mary chuckled at this.

"Have any of you seen Donal?" she asked.

"Nae," Mary said. "Lassies?"

"I haven't," Sophia said.

"Nor I," the youngest lass said.

The other young woman remained suspiciously silent. "Have you seen him?" Tina asked when the woman looked her way.

"Bethia, answer the lass," Mary scolded and then to Tina, "She's a wee bit shy."

"I havenae," she said then turned back to her work.

"Sorry we couldn't be more help," Mary gave her a sad smile then turned back to the stove.

So much for getting any info on Donal. Why couldn't she simply forget about him? It was obvious he wasn't the one for her. She finished her tea and bread, thanked Mary and headed back to her room.

Just as she was about to head upstairs, Ashley appeared. "How was your date?" she asked, her voice bubbling with excitement.

"Is that what it was?" Tina asked. She had to laugh at Ashley's eagerness.

"You know it was. Tell me all about it." She grabbed Tina's arm and yanked her into the great hall where they sat across from each other at one of the dining tables.

"Nothing exciting happened. They're both nice. Marcas doesn't seem interested in leaving Breaghacraig, so I think that rules him out. Jock is cute, but I don't know. I didn't feel any spark."

"And Tam?"

"Oh, I don't feel like I really had a chance to talk to him with all the commotion last night."

"I know! I can't believe Donal did that. Have you seen him today?"

"No. I was wondering if you had."

"He's probably embarrassed." Then she shook her head, "No. What am I saying? He's never embarrassed by any of the crazy things he does around here."

"You really don't care for him, do you? Why?"

Ashley became thoughtful at that, "I do like him, but I just don't think he's right for you." She paused, obviously weighing her words. "Living here is a bit like living in a small town. Everyone knows each other's business. Or they think they know, but in actual fact it's all just stuff that you hear. So, I've heard things about Donal being irresponsible and thoughtless. Not mean or cruel, just not the kind of guy I would have been friends with back home."

"Unfortunately, he feels that. He thinks no one around here likes him. Not you, or Jenna or anyone else for that matter."

"Really? The men like him, I think." Ashley's brow furrowed as she thought. "I mean, I've asked Cailin about him, but the guys never gossip about each other. It's not good for morale. They have to depend on each other when they're in the heat of battle, so they'd never say anything. They are very loyal to each other."

"I feel bad for him," Tina said.

"I wouldn't worry about Donal. He's a big boy. He can fend for himself."

"I'm not worried, but he's got a huge responsibility now that Elena's here."

"Responsibility has never been his strong suit, from what I've heard, but who knows maybe she's just what he needs to find it."

"I hope so."

"Let's not talk about him anymore. I think we should set up a date for you and Tam. What do you think?"

"Oh, I don't know. I think I'm done. Maybe this was a bad idea."

"Don't say that. Edna wouldn't have sent you if she didn't have something in mind. It'll happen, you'll see."

∼

Tina sat in front of the hearth in her room wondering why she couldn't get Donal off her mind. Ashley was right. He wasn't the one for her, but none of the other men were either. She stared into the flames and tried to clear her mind of anything to do with meeting her match.

"Tina?" Edna's voice came from the fire, just as Wallace said it did.

Tina sat bolt upright, not saying a word. The room felt different, like it was filled with static electricity.

"I know yer there, lass. I can see ye."

"You can?" Tina peered into the fire thinking she'd see Edna's face, but all she saw were the flames.

"Yes. Now, I know yer having some doubts about our Donal."

Tina felt a weight lift from her, "So, he is the one you wanted me to meet."

"He is and he's perfect for ye."

"I don't know about that." Tina wished she felt as confident as Edna sounded.

"Ye don't have to know, ye just have to feel. How do ye feel about him?"

Tina put her logic in her back pocket and thought about what Edna said. "I like him."

"And?"

"And nothing." Edna remained quiet and as the silence stretched, Tina had to admit to herself that wasn't true. "He makes me feel butterflies, which I haven't felt since my high school days. And that was a long time ago."

When Edna spoke again, her voice was gentle and encouraging.

"Give him a chance. Ye believed in me enough to let me send ye back there, now believe that I ken what I'm doing."

Tina found herself wanting to believe in Edna. She thought back to her excitement about traveling to the past, about the looks of love she had seen between Hamish and Elle, Ashley and Cailin, and the others Edna had matched. She wanted that, she really did, so she needed to treat this like her other projects. She needed to see this through the tough times. "I'll try. Ashley and Jenna keep trying to set me up with other men."

"I know. They're not for ye. Tell Ashley not to worry, I'll find someone else for them," Edna said. "Ye need someone who'd be willing to come back to yer own time with ye."

"True." That was an absolute fact because there was no way she was staying in this time.

"Donal is the one," Edna's reassuring voice was telling her exactly what she'd needed to hear.

Well that was one big question answered for her. It wasn't her only hesitation, though. "I'm worried about his temper. It frightened me."

"I'm not excusing his outburst, but ye need to remember that he didn't hurt Marcas. The warriors fight and spar under friendly conditions all the time and that can look violent when ye aren't used to it. He let his jealousy get the better of him last night and he feels ashamed fer it."

"You know about that?" Tina couldn't even begin to wrap her brain around how that was possible.

"I know more than ye think I do. Now, what he did was wrong, but he knows it and he won't do it again. At least I hope he won't."

Tina threw her hands in the air, "That's not terribly reassuring, Edna."

"This is all new to him. He's never been in love before."

"He's in love with me?" Tina was shocked to hear this. They'd only known each other a few days, but she'd managed to develop strong feelings for him pretty quickly. One thing she was sure of was that it wasn't love. Not yet.

"I believe so. If not, it's only a matter of time."

"But, I thought he was using me. He told Jock and Marcas he just wanted me to raise his daughter."

"Ye met him on a verra challenging day, ye must admit. He wasnae thinking straight. Yes, he may have seen ye as an answer to his childcare problem in that moment, but relationships can evolve. No one would react the way he did over losing a nanny. He was afraid of losing something much more important, someone he really cares about."

She clutched her belly. The butterflies were back along with a strange sensation she hadn't had about a guy in a long time. Hope.

"Now, promise me ye'll give him a chance and tell Ashley I said that she needs to stop trying to do my job. She's nae a matchmaker."

"I'll tell her before she sets up another date with Tam."

"Good. Say hello to everyone for me."

"I will."

The charged atmosphere in the room changed and Tina knew she was alone again. Her doubts about Donal were still there, but she trusted Edna and she was willing to do as she had asked. She'd give him another chance. She was more determined than ever to find him now.

Avoiding Tina wasn't the best plan, but Donal was embarrassed by his recent behavior with Marcas. He hadn't seen her since the embarrassing incident in the great hall, but he was aware that she'd spent some time yesterday with Marcas and Jock. It bothered him more than he wished to admit, but he could understand it. He'd seen the horrified look on her face when he'd gone after Marcas and was sure she now thought of him as the brute he truly was. He would apologize to her when he saw her, but that would be it. He would no longer delude himself with the thought that she might be the one for him. The one woman he never believed existed, before he met her.

His heart had been battered and he didn't know what was going to become of him. Finding out about Elena had been a shock, but he wanted to be the da she deserved. He had never expected to fall for a woman and now that he had messed that up he didn't know how to search for a mother. He certainly didn't deserve a good woman in his life, even though Elena did.

He'd made a bad showing on the practice field this day. Marcas was angry with him and let him have it by putting every ounce of that anger into his sword and dirk. Luckily they weren't battling to the death, because Donal was sure he'd be dead now. He apologized to him and to Tam and Jock, all of whom said they would back off on their interest in Tina if he was truly looking at her for more than just a roll in the hay. He assured them he was. Not that it mattered, he was sure she wouldn't want anything to do with him now that she'd seen what an arse he could be. It had been a rough time since that night and he wasn't proud of himself for what happened. He dropped his head to his chest as he made his way to the well where he poured a cool bucket of water over his head. He shook the water out of his hair and rubbed it from his face.

"Looks refreshing," Tina said, from behind him.

The sound of her voice hit him in the gut. He turned slowly to see her smiling warmly at him. Saints be praised. It didn't appear she was angry with him, but he'd better be sure of it. "Tina."

"I've been looking for you," she said.

"I didn't think ye'd ever want to see me again."

"I wasn't sure I did."

"Tina, I want to apologize for my behavior the other night. I was jealous that ye were laughing with Tam. What I did was wrong. Can ye forgive me?"

"I can, because you were man enough to admit you did something you shouldn't have."

Relief swept over him. He felt lighter than he had in two days. It welled up from inside of him.

"I do have one question for you, though."

The hope disappeared. Maybe she'd forgiven him, but still didn't want him. "Jock and Marcas told me that the only reason you were interested in me was so I could be a mother to Elena. Is that true?"

Damn it! He couldn't believe they'd told her that. He plunked himself down on the edge of the well. Logan had told him to use his words. He was much better with a sword and dirk, but he was going to have to tell her something. Deciding that honesty was his best path forward, he took a deep breath and spoke to the ground at her feet. "It *was* true." He scanned her face for a reaction, but there was none, so he barreled on. "I thought ye'd be a good mother to her and I admit that at first that was my only interest." He hurried to continue, willing her to believe him. "But as I've gotten to know ye, my heart has opened to ye. Ye are more than I deserve and everything I want."

She didn't say anything and that made him nervous, but after a moment she surprised him by moving closer. So close in fact that the heat of her body sent waves of her intoxicating scent wafting over him. He sat perfectly still, not wanting to do anything that might cause her to move away. She placed her hand on his chest. "My heart is yours," she said before leaning in to kiss him.

Donal had never in all his years felt so unprepared. Her kiss was soft and sweet. He placed his hand on her waist and pulled her closer. Neither of them cared that they were in the middle of the courtyard where everyone could see them. It was as if they were alone in their own little world where the only thing that mattered was the tenderness they felt for each other.

Tina pulled back just enough to gaze into his eyes before leaning her forehead on his. "That was amazing," she said.

"Aye," was about all he could manage.

She glanced around and seemed to realize they weren't alone. "I should go."

"No. Please. Not yet." He looked down at his kilt and Tina did the same.

"Oh!" she squealed. "I'll stay right where I am, or maybe I should move back."

"Right where ye are is fine, lass." Having her so close was not going to help, but he needed to know she was real, that this was real. He would never have imagined his day would be this good.

"Okay. How's Elena?" she asked.

"She's with Doreen. She has been sleeping well, as I am sure ye know. I was going to get her now that I'm done." He looked into her eyes and saw his future. She would be his.

"Looks like you've got a bruise on your cheek." Her fingers gently touched his face.

He removed her hand. "That isnae helping," he said.

"Sorry. I wasn't thinking." She giggled at him and his heart took flight.

"Would ye like to come with me to get Elena?"

She nodded.

"I think it's safe now." He stood and they both glanced down.

Tina started to laugh and didn't seem able to stop herself.

"Oh, I see. Ye ken 'tis nae something to laugh at."

"I wouldn't know," she said, a teasing glint in her eye.

He leaned in close to get another whiff of her perfume and growled into her ear, "Mayhap I'll show ye later and then ye'll see why ye shouldnae laugh."

He was surprised when Tina punched him in the arm and gave him a shove, continuing to laugh. He did the only thing he could think to do at that moment. He put an arm around her shoulder and pulled her in. Tina wrapped her arm around his waist and together they walked through the courtyard until they came to Ashley McBain standing square in their way.

"Tina!" she said, with a disapproving scowl.

"Edna says you should mind your own business," Tina said. "And she says hello."

Ashley stood mouth agape, obviously struck speechless by Tina's comment.

"Donal, I'm going to stay and talk with Ashley if you don't mind. I'll see you later."

She kissed him on the cheek and he walked away with a lightness in his step and a warm hope in his heart.

CHAPTER 10

All the thoughts of wives and children that had been giving him a headache vanished magically when Tina forgave him. Once again, he could begin to imagine a new life, not just for himself but for Elena as well. The sound of a crying bairn caught his attention and as he scanned the courtyard he saw that Doreen was heading his way with a wailing Elena.

"I think she's sick," she said. "She feels warm to me." Her wrinkled brow and a slight shake of her head worried Donal. "I must go. Ma is waiting for me."

He was ill prepared to be a da, but he was even more lacking in this area. He had no idea what to do with a sick child. Doreen handed his daughter to him.

"I think her teeth are coming in," he called to Doreen's back as she walked away. He hoped that was all it was. He placed the back of his hand on her forehead, as he'd seen his mother do when he was a young lad. Elena did feel warm, but if she had a fever what was he to do? Her wailing continued as he held her close and went back to his room. Along the way he looked for the ladies of the castle, hoping for some help, but they were nowhere to be seen. If he could just get her to sleep, then he could go in search of someone who might know what to do.

He lay her on the bed and tried everything he could to get her to stop, but nothing he did worked. He picked her up, rocking her and pacing back and forth across the room. Nothing he had seen Tina do was working. Fear gripped him. What if she were to die? What if she had whatever illness had killed her mother? No. Fate would not be so cruel as to bring his daughter into his life and then snatch her away so fast. He would do anything to make her better. He held her closer. "Shhhh, sweetling. Go to sleep. Da is here. I will take care of ye."

∽

"Did Edna really say that?" Ashley asked, watching her daughter Emma plucking blades of grass along the roadside as they walked. Her son was contently cradled against her chest.

"She did," Tina replied. She shouldn't feel so happy about upsetting Ashley, but she'd had one of the best kisses of her life today so happiness was all around her.

"I'm not so sure I agree with her, but I'll stay out of it and I'll tell Jenna as well."

"I really like him," Tina said. "Don't ask me why, because I can't quite put my finger on it. There's just something there."

"Do you mind that he has a child?"

"No, not at all. Elena is a sweet little girl who needs a mother and I'd be happy to fill that spot. And before you say anything, Donal admitted to me that at first he only saw me as the answer to his prayers. Elena needed a mother and Donal had no experience being a father."

"And you believe him."

Why was she so skeptical? "Yes, I do."

"Okay. I won't say anything else about it." Emma presented her mother with a bouquet of grass. "Thank you, sweetie. It's beautiful." Emma smiled and went back to work picking more grass. Ashley turned to Tina. "I want you to know I'm happy for you. I'm happy you found what you were looking for. How are you going to convince him to go back with you?"

"I don't know. I don't think it's going to be a problem, though."

"Well, let me know if you need any help or if you need to contact Edna."

"I will."

"Tam will be disappointed when I tell him."

"I think Donal got that all straightened out with them today."

"He didn't start a brawl did he?"

"I don't think so. It looks like he got the raw end of whatever happened though."

"Emma, let's go back," Ashley said, holding out her hand for her daughter.

Tina couldn't wait to get back to Breaghacraig. She wanted to see Donal and Elena. They were going to be her family and she couldn't wait to take them home with her to meet her mother and father. They would be surprised, but she knew they would also be welcoming. As they neared the gates, Tina noticed Doreen hurrying their way.

"Doreen!" she called.

"I must hurry. Ma is waiting." She practically ran up to them. "I think Elena is sick. She has a fever."

"Oh, no!" Tina said as Doreen ran past them on her way home. "I'd better hurry."

"Go on. It's going to take us a while to get there," Ashley said.

Tina lifted her skirts and ran all the way through the courtyard, then the castle doors and up the stairs to Donal's chamber. She tapped lightly and opened the door to find a sight that was so sweet it brought happy tears to her eyes. Donal lay on the bed with Elena on his chest. They were both sound asleep. There was something about seeing a big, tough guy tenderly holding a sweet little one that melted her heart. She found an extra plaid folded over the back of a chair and brought it to the bed to cover them both before seating herself by the fire and waiting for one or both of them to stir.

A short time later, Ashley tapped on the door before coming in. "Is she alright?" she whispered.

"I don't know. They were sleeping when I got here and I didn't want to disturb them."

"I brought you something to give her in case she has a fever. You'll have to keep close watch though. If it gets really bad, we'll have to contact Edna. Dr Ferguson is on his way to deliver the babies, but I have no idea when he's going to get here."

"Where did you get this?" Tina asked holding up the bottle of liquid children's medicine.

"Edna. It was in the basket of goodies you brought with you."

"Goodness, she thinks of everything."

Ashley headed for the door. "I'm going to keep my distance until we know she's okay. I don't want to expose my little ones to whatever it is that she has. Jenna will want to do the same. I'll tell the others. We don't want the pregnant ladies to catch anything either."

"We'll just quarantine her up here then."

"I'll make sure you have everything you need."

"Thank you."

"I love that," Ashley said, pointing to Donal and Elena sleeping on the bed.

Tina's heart swelled at the sight of them, "Me, too."

∼

Donal opened his eyes and was surprised to see Tina seated by the fire. "Tina, you're here."

"Doreen told me she thought Elena was sick."

"I cannae tell. She was fussing and crying until I got her to sleep. She felt warm to me, but I cannae say if she's sick."

Tina came to the bedside and placed her hand delicately on Elena's forehead, trying not to disturb her. "We'll keep an eye on her," Tina whispered.

"We? Ye mean ye'll stay here with us?"

JENNAE VALE

"That's what I mean. I'm not going to desert you when you need me."

He took her hand and brought it to his lips. "I do need ye, lass. I dinnae ken what to do for her."

"Ashley gave me some medicine to give her. It might help."

"Should we wake her?"

"No. We'll wait. She seems comfortable there with you."

He shifted Elena on his chest.

"Do you want me to take her?" she asked.

"I would like to sit up," he replied.

Tina adjusted the pillows so he could sit up a bit. Despite the movement, Elena didn't stir. "My brother has little ones and they get sick all the time, so don't worry. She'll be alright."

"Do ye believe so? I lost more than one brother and sister to the fever when I was a bairn."

"I hadn't thought about that," Tina frowned. "We don't know what she's sick with. Hopefully it's nothing serious."

"What will we do if it is?" She could hear the panic in his voice and knew he needed reassurance. She took his hand in hers and squeezed it.

"Ashley said there's a doctor coming to help Helene and Sara give birth. Hopefully he'll be here soon. If not, we can depend on Edna to help us."

"The witch?"

"That's the one."

Donal didn't know much about witches. The only thing he'd ever heard about them was that they were bad. Tina sat next to him on the bed and placed Elena beside him. "Don't look so worried," she said as she rubbed her fingers across his forehead. "Relax."

He took her hands in his. "Thank ye, Tina."

"Of course, you're both important to me."

He liked the sound of that. He was important to someone. He was important to her. He was happy to have a partner in Tina. Someone he knew would be there for him and for Elena. He'd always resented his parents because they had been too busy with all this brothers and sisters to notice him. In the short time he'd had a child of his own, he had seen how much work it took to care for a child, never mind eight children. They must have gone through so much worry. Where would their next meal come from, what would happen if they were sick? It had been so hard for them and he hadn't realized it.

He had been so wrapped up in his own little world that he hadn't seen the sacrifices they'd made for their children. When they'd fostered him out, he thought it was because they didn't want him anymore, but now he understood it was to make sure he was well cared for and that some day he'd have a better life than the one they'd had. That's what he wanted to do for Elena. He wanted her life to be a good one with much promise of brighter days to come.

"I'm going to go down to the kitchen. Maybe Mary has some chicken broth for Elena. I'll bring something for you, too," she said.

How his luck had changed. From nothing going right in his life to having everything good he could possibly imagine right here in this room with him.

"I'll be right back," Tina said.

"We'll be here waiting for ye."

~

Mary wasn't in the kitchen when Tina entered, the only one there was Bethia. "Where is everyone?" Tina asked.

Bethia seemed quite unsure of herself, but managed to answer, "The great hall."

"Where else would they be?" Tina smiled. She hoped to put Bethia at ease. She wasn't sure why the young woman seemed so tentative around her. "I was wondering if I could get some broth for Elena. She's not feeling well."

"Aye. Mary made some today." The girl kept her head down as she worked and Tina remembered Mary saying she was shy.

"And can you put together some food for Donal?"

Bethia gave her a sideways glance before nodding her head. "His luck's nae been good of late."

JENNAE VALE

Tina was surprised to hear Bethia try to start a conversation with her.

"I know. It's not bad enough that he's lost his wife, but then to find out he had a child the way that he did."

"Wife?" Bethia asked, fumbling with her apron.

"Yes. Sionaid. I think she used to work here."

"They werenae married," Bethia said as she puttered around the kitchen grabbing a basket, then a napkin to line it. "He didnae even ken her name."

Tina was shocked. "Are you sure?"

"I am. Donal likes the ladies, but tires of them quickly. A few weeks after Sionaid spent time with Donal, she went home to her family."

"Did she say why?" Tina asked to her back.

Bethia gathered a bowl and two cups from a high shelf. "Nae. She didnae tell any of us, but I'm nae surprised. He'd already moved on to someone else, a tavern girl from the village. Tara? Tilly?"

"Tess?" Tina asked.

"Yes, I think that was it. Then there was Isla, her father is a fisherman. And then Ava, she sells fabric and does sewing."

"How do you know all this?"

"I've eyes in me head. Before ye came it was me he wanted. I knew he would get around to me eventually. He is sweet and verra handsome but everyone knows he isnae serious about anyone or anything, really." She shrugged. "Nothing happened between us. I had to go home for a few days and I'm happy I did. I cannae afford to be with child. I feel terrible that Sionaid passed. She was a good friend and we laughed a lot."

Tina didn't know what to say. Donal had lied to her. The happiness she'd felt a short time ago vanished to be replaced by a gut wrenching feeling of betrayal. Donal was turning out to be the type of guy she'd avoid at all costs back home. She didn't need a man who used women until he tired of them. Tina didn't want to be another notch on his bedpost. She had some thinking to do. It was obvious to her now that she couldn't be with a man who had not only lied to her about being married, but was the worst kind of womanizer. He'd had plenty of chances to tell her the truth and he'd chosen not to. She had no idea what Edna had been thinking. She could not be with Donal, not now. She would focus on Elena. It wasn't her fault her father was a player. She would stick around to make sure Elena was going to be okay, then she was going home. Alone.

"Here ye are," Bethia said, handing her a basket. "Be careful with the broth. Dinnae spill it." She smiled at Tina and for the first time seemed to realize the impact her words had. She looked very uncomfortable.

Tina needed to stop her hands from shaking. She pulled in a long, slow breath, closed her eyes and willed them to be still. "Thank you, Bethia. I'll be careful." She seemed a sweet girl who'd obviously been caught in Donal's web of deceit.

"I'm sorry that ye didnae know."

"I do now. Thank you."

She couldn't remember her walk back to Donal's room because her head was spinning. How many women had there been before she'd arrived? Were there anymore surprises about Donal that she'd discover? She took a deep breath before opening the door and entering his room.

"Yer back," Donal said, popping up from the bed to take the basket from her hands.

"Be careful. There's broth in there." Her voice was devoid of emotion. She simply had to control herself or she'd start to yell and that was the last thing she wanted to do. Elena was tucked into the cradle with blankets. Her little cheeks were pink but she seemed to be sleeping peacefully.

"Is everything alright, lass?" he asked.

"No." She took a moment to compose herself before speaking again. "No, it's not."

"What's happened?" He put the basket down on the table and came back to take her hands, which she yanked away. She didn't want him to touch her. If he did she might lose her resolve and she couldn't afford that.

"You lied to me," she said, stuffing down the urge to scream at him.

"What do ye mean?" He seemed honestly baffled by her accusation, but she knew better.

"You told me you were married and you weren't." Adrenaline pumped through her body and the shaking returned. She folded her arms across her chest and tucked her hands under her arms where they wouldn't give her away.

"I... never said I was married. Ye assumed I was," he said without raising his voice.

"You should have told me I was wrong, but you didn't." The words tasted bitter as she spoke them. This was too much, he was making excuses for his behavior.

"I needed ye to help me. I thought if ye felt bad for me it would be easier." His eyes seemed to plead with her to believe him.

"Easier to what? To fool me into falling for you? To get me to marry you?" All the hurt and disappointment she was feeling were in those questions.

"I told ye I was desperate when I first met ye. I admit, I tried to take advantage of the situation, but I know who ye are now and I've already apologized."

"Here I was feeling bad for you. You couldn't even remember her name." She bit down on her bottom lip hoping to disguise the hurt coursing through her body with every beat of her heart.

"Who's name?"

"Sionaid!" she yelled.

"How do ye know all this?" He scrubbed his hands through his hair, all color draining from his face.

"Bethia," she said.

"Och! Nae."

"Och! Aye," Tina said, purposely using the Scottish terms. "Maybe the reason Tess was so rude the other day is that she heard about Isla. Or maybe she and one of your many women had been talking. How many other little Donals are running around?"

He stared at her not speaking.

"I asked you a question. Do you have any other children?" She choked out the words through gritted teeth.

He shrugged his shoulders and turned away from her.

"What is that supposed to mean?"

"It means I dinnae know."

"You don't know?"

"Nae. I didnae ken Sionaid was with child. She didnae tell me." His voice was quiet, almost inaudible. "I never thought to check on the others. I havenae been an honorable man, I ken it. I thought we were having a bit of fun, is all. I didnae mean to hurt anyone."

"You're digging yourself a deep hole," she said, vindication in her anger.

"I'm nae digging a hole. I'm telling ye the truth." He turned back to her, outstretched hands pleading with her.

"Why should I believe you? You've been lying to me all along. All those things you said yesterday about opening your heart to me were lies. I am nothing but a bit of fun to you."

"I wasnae lying!" he shouted.

Elena stirred and began to cry. Tina tore her eyes from Donal's lying face and went to her. "Come here, sweetie. It's alright."

"I wasnae lying," he said in a softer tone. Tina felt her resolve threatening to crack at the pain in his voice.

Tina kissed Elena's forehead. She was not going to listen to another word he said, no matter what. She would focus on seeing Elena better. It was her only project now. "You *are* very warm. I'm going to give her some medicine. It should make her fever go down." She lay Elena on her back and filled the dropper from the medicine bottle with the red liquid. "Here you go, baby." She slipped the dropper between Elena's lips and was surprised she took it without a fight. Her brother's kids were much more difficult to medicate. They had to physically hold them down to get anything into them. "Now, shall we try some broth?"

Donal took the broth from the basket and retrieved her little spoon. Tina didn't look at him. She couldn't. She was so hurt and disappointed that she wanted to cry, but she wouldn't. She'd save that for later when she was alone in her room. Elena refused to eat. And began to whimper weakly. "I'm concerned. Something's not right."

"What could it be?" Donal asked.

"I don't know, but there's not much left for us to do. Let the medicine take effect. I'm going back to my room. If you need me, come get me." She put Elena back in the cradle and gently rocked her, she fell immediately back to sleep. Tina wasn't sure what was wrong with her. It could be the flu, which should be manageable, but with a young child like Elena, it could be disastrous. She wasn't sure she should leave Elena alone with Donal, but so far he'd proven to at least be a concerned father even if he was a lying cheat of a man. Tina would need her sleep if, as she suspected, she would be awakened in the middle of the night to take care of her.

"Tina, please, stay. We have much to speak of. Please dinnae be angry with me."

"It's a little late for that." She closed the door behind her before slumping against the wall feeling as though her heart had been ripped from her chest.

CHAPTER 11

She had no idea how long she'd been asleep before the sound of Elena crying woke her, sending her running to Donal's room. She opened the door to find him walking the floor with her.

"There now, wee one. 'Tis alright. Yer Da is here," he spoke softly and soothingly to her as she rested her head on his chest.

Once again, Tina was reminded that despite his lack of experience and his sudden fatherhood, he was doing his best to be a good father.

"Have you had any sleep?" she asked.

"Nae. I've had much on me mind. I'm worried for Elena." He sounded a bit defensive, but she couldn't worry about that just now.

"I'll take her back to my room. You should lie down and try to sleep."

"Nae. I'm her Da. I'll take care of her," he stubbornly said.

Tina sat on the edge of the bed. "You don't have to prove anything to me."

"I'm nae trying to prove anything to ye. I'm proving it to meself."

"Is she still hot?" Tina asked.

"I dinnae believe so."

"See if she'll drink some water." Ashley and Jenna had assured her that the well water for the castle was safe to drink. She filled a small cup and brought it to Elena. Holding it up to her lips, she was pleased when Elena took a few sips. She rested the back of her hand on the child's forehead and was satisfied that the fever had gone down. "Maybe if we're lucky it'll be gone in the morning."

"I pray 'tis so," he said.

The tension in the air between them was palpable, but there was no way to resolve it. He wasn't the man she'd thought and she knew that it was unlikely he'd change. So, in her mind there was absolutely no reason to give in to the things her heart was telling her she should. "Before I go back to my room let me give her a little more medicine. It's been long enough since her last dose."

Once again, Tina was pleased that Elena took the medicine easily. She gave her another sip of water before gently cupping the child's face in her hand. "Good night, sweetie. I hope you're feeling better in the morning."

She didn't look at Donal and without either of them saying a word, she returned to her own room hoping the rest of the night would pass without incident.

Cracking the door just a bit, Tina checked in to see how Elena was doing. Both she and Donal were sound asleep. The fever seemed to be gone, but she knew it could come back with a vengeance later in the day. Gathering the basket from last night she headed downstairs. "How are you feeling this morning?" Ashley asked.

"Like I was hit by a truck," she said. "I had a fight with Donal last night and that coupled with Elena being sick really has me feeling hopeless."

"I'm sorry," Ashley said. "Can I help?"

"I don't think so. All I can do is hope that Elena gets well quickly so I can go home. I don't want to stay here anymore."

Ashley appeared sad to hear this. "When you're ready to go, just tell me and I'll contact Edna."

"Do you think she'll let me leave without Donal?" Tina asked, adding a new worry to the already long list of things upsetting her.

"She's not going to make you stay here. Or at least I don't think she will," Ashley said.

What would she do if Edna refused to send her home? What could she do? She had a sick feeling in the pit of her stomach.

"You should eat something. We've all noticed you haven't been enjoying the food."

"Well, at least if I'm stuck here I'll probably starve to death, putting me out of my misery."

"Don't say that," Ashley protested. "You're not going to starve to death. And it's not so bad here. Some of us actually love our home."

"I didn't mean to insult the place. It's just not for me. I miss my family. This is the first time I've been away on my own. I guess I need them more than I thought." After years of feeling jealous of Elle and having that wedge driven between them because of her fame, the time they'd spent together on tour had given them an opportunity to get reacquainted and to be friends again. She wished more than anything she had Elle or her mom around to talk with about all of this.

"While you're here, we're your family. You can rely on us just like you were at home."

"I know. I'm sorry. I'm just in such an awful place emotionally right now. I don't know what to do."

"What could be so wrong that you can't work it out with him? What did he do?"

"He let me believe Sionaid had been his wife. He lied to me."

"They weren't married? I'm so sorry. We were all shocked to hear that he had a wife, I guess that's why."

"He admitted that when I first arrived he would have done or said anything to get me to help with the baby, but we moved past that, I thought. He had plenty of time to come clean and tell me the truth but he didn't. And not only that, I found out she probably didn't tell him about the baby because he had already moved on to another conquest. He is nothing but a player and I don't need someone like that in my life."

"Oh, Tina. That is awful."

"I guess you were right all along," Tina said. "He wasn't the right one for me."

"Tina, I don't want to be right about this. I saw your feelings for him grow and if there's one thing I do know, it's if you think there was something there, something that attracted you, then you shouldn't let that go so easily."

"I don't know if I can trust him. How long until I am just tossed aside like those other women?"

"I know. I'm not excusing that. What I am saying is talk to him about it. Talk until you don't think you can talk anymore. It is completely possible for people to learn from their mistakes."

"I've been lied to so many times by guys. I would have to worry everyday that he wasn't being honest, that he didn't want me any more. How can I ever trust him again?"

"Have you ever lied to someone? I know I have. Or have you ever lied by omission?"

Tina thought about that for a moment. She knew what Ashley was getting at. "Of course I've lied. We all have."

"So, does that mean that everyone should cut you from their lives? Does that mean that you can never be trusted? I get it, Donal has a history. But that doesn't mean he wants to be that guy forever. He never found a person he wanted to change for, maybe now he has."

"I know what you're trying to do and I appreciate it, but in this case, I'm not so sure I can just let this go."

"I think if you hold every man you ever meet to such a high standard, you're always going to be disappointed. That's all I'm going to say."

That hit pretty close to home. Tina knew she had high standards when it came to men. Was there something wrong with that? Maybe there was. It could be the reason she'd never had a serious romance. Not one. She wanted so much to be part of a couple. To have someone to share her life with and yet Tina wasn't sure she could change or that she should.

"I'm going to bring this back to the kitchen," Tina said. "I'll talk to you later."

If it was possible, she walked away from Ashley feeling even worse than she had before. Why was it that once she'd dug her heels in it was impossible for her to do anything but keep digging? She thought about all the times she'd cut men loose because their motives weren't what she thought they should be. When was the last time she'd had more than two dates with the same guy? Wasn't that why she was here? Self-reflection wasn't her strong suit. She had a very hard time admitting when she was wrong and so she almost never did.

Mary was hard at work, as always. "Good morning," she said, placing the basket on the table.

"Good morn to ye, lass. How's the babe?"

"She was cool to the touch this morning, but I'm worried the fever will come back later in the day."

"Aye. 'Tis good to be cautious. How's yer man, Donal holding up?"

"He's not my man and he was sleeping when I checked in on them."

"Poor thing. I ken I'm hard on him, but deep down he's a good man. I can see it when he's with ye and with the babe."

Hearing Mary's words warmed Tina's heart a bit. She knew Donal wasn't a terrible person, but with everything she now knew, it was making it very hard for her to see.

"I was wondering if you could put something together for me to bring back for them."

"And what of ye? Do ye never eat?"

"I'll have some of that good bread if you have any?"

"I've always got bread for ye. Do ye like fruit?"

"Yes, very much."

"Good. I've got apples and pears, will they do?"

"They will."

"Cooked oats?"

"Yes."

"I knew I would find something ye'd eat," Mary laughed as she hurried about the kitchen obviously thrilled about her new discovery.

JENNAE VALE

She filled the basket to the brim. "Ye'll be needing enough to last ye the day."

"Thank you, Mary. You've been so kind."

"I'd thank ye no' to say a word about it. I'd rather them think me mean," she chuckled.

"I think they might be on to you," Tina said. "They only say the nicest things about you."

"Do they now?" She smiled as she went back to work. "Off with ye, I've things to do."

Her interaction with Mary brought a warm smile to her face. Despite her protests, she was a very sweet lady and everyone knew it.

∼

He'd never been so worried about anything or anyone in his whole life. This was his daughter. He was going to care for her and protect her from harm to the best of his ability or he'd die trying. The relief he felt knowing that Elena's fever was gone was profound. Now that she was feeling better he could concentrate on trying to make things right with Tina.

He'd seen the hurt and disappointment in her eyes and heard it in her voice and he knew he'd done that to her. His guilt over lying and what a terrible man he had been was overwhelming him. He'd resigned himself to losing her once before but he didn't want that now. He wasn't the same man that had pursued those women. He knew, now, what it meant to find someone special and he didn't want to find someone else. He wanted Tina and he would do whatever was necessary to keep her. Logan told him to use his words and that is what he would do. He wasn't sure what he was going to say that might change her mind, but he would try.

The door opened and Tina entered. "I brought food. Mary thought you'd be hungry."

"Mary is right, as always." A crooked grin appeared on his lips. One he hoped would charm Tina. Donal had never cared enough about a woman to want to win her back, but Tina was different. When she walked through that door, his heart skipped a beat and his mind went to work. He had to find a way to let her know she was special to him. That he would do anything for her. "Are ye feeling better this morning? Ye were quite upset last night." Much to his surprise she didn't respond the way he'd hoped.

"I found out the man I thought I loved was a liar who steps on hearts without a second thought." She took a deep breath before continuing, her anger obvious. "That you not only didn't remember Sionaid's name, but had tossed her aside so fast you were already making your way through the women of the village. How long did your relationship with Tess last?"

Donal didn't say anything to that.

"Honestly, Donal, how long do you really think this," she wagged a finger back and forth between them, "is going to last? Clearly you are not a man familiar with commitment. I am not looking to be someone's throw away. I wanted..." she stopped and Donal didn't breathe until she spoke again. "I wanted to find someone that would love me for me. Someone who would be my partner in life. Obviously that person doesn't exist. Not in this time or in the future."

"Tina, that's not true. I..."

"What do you know about the truth, Donal?" That stopped him. He had lied or at least misled her about nearly everything from the moment he met her. But not about how he felt. For the first time in his life he had been completely honest about his feelings for a woman, but she didn't trust him and he couldn't blame her.

He'd merely asked a question. One he'd hoped showed his concern for her. Somehow he'd said the wrong thing and now she was angry. Or perhaps she was still angry. Despite all the women he'd known, he had no experience with this side of them.

"Forgive me. I didnae mean to rile ye, but it seems I cannae help myself."

She grumbled something under her breath as she unpacked the basket. He stood and walked to the table where as he reached for an apple his hand grazed hers. She froze and he noted she closed her eyes. This was a woman at war with herself. She still had feelings for him and yet she was denying them. He wanted to touch her, to hold her, to promise her he'd never lie to her again. If he did, would she reject him? As the seconds ticked by he realized he had no idea what to say to her. Maybe if he could keep her in the room his brain would kick in and figure out what he was supposed to say to fix this. He grabbed an apple from the basket and rubbed it on his plaid to have something to do. "Ye should eat," he said.

"I wish everyone would stop telling me to eat. I'll eat when I'm hungry," she snapped.

"As ye wish."

"*You* should eat and then go about your day. I'll stay here with Elena." When she glanced at him there was a sadness in her eyes that he hadn't seen before.

"Tina…"

She held up her hand to stop his approach and his words, "No, don't say anything. I'm trying my best to get through this. I am here to help take care of Elena. When she's feeling better, I'm going home. So, until then we are nothing more than two people who care about one little girl."

What could he say to that? They were not to be. He grabbed some bread, cheese and the apple and left the room. He was angry with himself for the lies, his careless past, and his idjit brain that couldnae think of the right thing to say to her. She'd seemed touched by his plight and he'd shamelessly taken advantage of her kind heart. He truly was as awful as she thought him to be.

~

At around the noon hour Tina got some relief. Doreen came back and offered to stay with Elena for a while.

"She's been sleeping quite a bit, but at least she seems comfortable. Send for me if she seems worse."

"Aye. Me ma tells me many of the villagers are sick with the same. 'Tis never a good thing. We'll lose many to be sure."

Remembering where she was and when she was had a sobering

effect on her. A bad feeling worked its way through her. What if Elena was one of those who would be lost? "Let's hope it doesn't come to that." Tina vowed to herself that she wouldn't allow that to happen. "Maybe I should stay here with her."

"She'll be fine for a short while. Ye need some time out of this room."

She gave Elena one last kiss on the forehead and was satisfied that she no longer had a fever, "I won't be far if you need me."

Once outside in the courtyard, Tina lifted her face to the sun, feeling its warmth chase away the chill she felt inside. How could this have happened? She'd been sent here to find a mate and somehow the idyllic scenes she had imagined when she first thought about it in her own time, were far from the reality she was living here and now. Why did Edna send her? Was it because she knew Elena would need her?

She found herself walking towards the practice field. She wasn't sure why, but for some reason she needed to see Donal. Not to speak with him, but just to know he was there. She watched him from afar greatly appreciating his skill and was struck by how attracted to him she still was. He spun around suddenly and was facing her direction, he must have seen her because he spoke to his opponent and began striding her way.

Tina pivoted on her heel, heading away from the field and Donal.

"Tina!" he called.

She didn't answer as she hurried on her way.

"Tina!" he was right behind her now and it was implausible that she couldn't hear him. She stopped where she was. "Is it Elena? Is she well?"

"She's fine. She seems better."

"I saw ye and was afeared something was wrong. I'm relieved to hear yer news."

What a fool she was. It wasn't her he wanted to see. He was worried for his daughter, as he should be. "Sorry. I didn't mean to scare you."

"Who's with her?" he asked, placing his dirk back in its sheath.

"Doreen came back today. I told her I'd only be gone a short while.

I should go back." He was too close. She needed to get away from him so she could breathe. She turned and began to walk away.

"I'll walk with ye," he said, hurrying to catch up with her.

"No need. You should go back to what you were doing." She couldn't look at him as she kept walking.

"I wish to see my daughter. I'm coming with ye." His patience seemed to be wearing thin and she realized she may have pushed him too far. Maybe he was more affected by her than she gave him credit for.

As he walked along beside her, Tina was acutely aware of him. The way he slowed his stride to stay at her side, the sheen of sweat on his shirtless chest and arms. She found herself breathless and aroused by him and yet confused and uncertain about where these emotions were coming from. Hadn't she already made up her mind about him? He didn't try to apologize as he had before. In fact he didn't speak at all. Any conversation, any move at all would have to come from her.

He opened the castle doors allowing her to walk in before him, being the type of gentleman she'd always hoped for and not the type of guy who let the door slam in your face before you got through it. Then he stopped at the bottom of the stairs waiting for her to go first.

"I'm going to look for Ashley," she said. "I'll be up in a little while." The need to escape his incredible pull on her was great. If she didn't create some distance between them she might find herself in his arms once again and she couldn't let that happen. Not yet and maybe not ever.

He bounded up the stairs two at a time and out of sight. Tina stood at the bottom looking up for a long while after he was gone.

CHAPTER 12

"Are you alright?" Sara asked, surprising Tina as she stood at the foot of the stairs.

"Yes," Tina said, recovering. "How are you?" Sara looked like she was ready to pop at any moment.

"Logan doesn't want me to be home alone during the day, so he brought me here this morning. I was looking for you."

"I'm right here," Tina said. "Did you need me for something?"

"No. I just wanted to spend some time with you." Sara's sweet smile lit up her whole face.

"Really?" Tina wasn't sure she should believe her.

"Yes, of course. Why wouldn't I?"

"I don't know. Maybe because I'm not Elle." She had to stop letting those old feelings of not being good enough get in the way.

"You're here. She's not. Don't get me wrong. I'm a huge fan of hers, but I really like you."

"You do?" There was that disbelief again.

"Wait, don't tell me. You've been living in your sister's shadow your whole life and you have a hard time believing anyone would want to get to know who *you* are."

JENNAE VALE

Tina's lips turned up for the first time in a while. Sara was someone she could call friend. "How'd you guess?"

"I've seen it on your face every time someone brings her up."

Tina was surprised by that. Could everyone see it, or was it just Sara? "I didn't know I was that transparent."

"Well, you are," Sara laughed. "How's Elena? I hear she's been sick."

"Fingers crossed she's on the road to recovery. Her fever's gone." She was relieved to have at least one thing off her plate. Of course, that meant it was time for her to go home. She decided not to think about that right now, after all, the fever could come back and Elena would need her then.

"Oh, good. I was worried about her."

"Do you worry about having a baby in this time?" Tina was concerned for Sara. She didn't want to frighten her, but things could go from bad to worse in a heartbeat.

"A little, but Edna won't let anything happen to us. And Logan has agreed to go back with me if I ever want to."

"That's sweet of him." *It must be nice to have a man in your life that you could count on,* she thought.

"Now you know why I love him. He's a good man," Sara said, rubbing her belly as she began to waddle away. "You know who else is a good man? Donal. Are you coming? I need to sit down." Sara plopped herself down in one of the chairs by the fire.

Tina wasn't sure she wanted to hear what came next, but she liked Sara and knew she should hear her out.

"I'm a pretty good judge of character, you know," Sara said.

"I get the feeling you're trying to tell me something," Tina laughed.

"And you've got good intuition," Sara replied.

"I don't know what you mean." Tina was truly puzzled by her statement. How could Sara know any such thing about her?

"I mean that you know… you feel, what's right for you. I think you know Donal is your man. You can fight it all you want and yes, I heard all about the lie and the other women, but give the guy a break. First of all, we have all done things that we might not be proud of. Second, if he had any idea that Sionaid was pregnant he would have married her for real."

"Are you always this direct," Tina asked.

"I have a tendency to say whatever's on my mind. It's not always a good thing," she giggled. "One more thing, since I seem to be on a roll here. Donal's whole life was turned upside down this week. He made some bad choices, but I don't think he was really in a position to make good ones."

Tina thought about that. It felt like they had spent a lot of time together, but in reality it was only a few days. He was trying so hard to figure out how to be a dad, maybe she was asking a lot to think that he could figure out how to be a partner at the same time.

"Hey, when you go back would you do me a favor? Would you give a letter to my brother?"

"Of course," Tina said. "I'd be happy to."

"Great. She put her hand in her skirt pocket and pulled out two envelopes."

Tina gazed at them. "What's in the other envelope?"

"It's the recipe for the tea. I really think you should do something with it."

"Wow! Thank you. I just might."

"The only thing I ask is that you call it Ayla's blend."

"I can do that."

"Good. I also made some other notes about things you could sell that are from this time. Don't worry, it's not my muffin recipe."

"You're quite the character, Sara. Here you are ready to give birth at any moment and you're thinking about me and Ayla's tea."

"I have to keep myself busy so I won't start to worry," she said and then leaning in, whispered, "I'm a little scared."

"Understandable," Tina replied. "I think I would be too. I hear there's a doctor coming to help you and Helene."

"Dr. Ferguson. He's delivered babies for Ashley and Jenna. Not Ashley's first. She did that all by herself with the help of one of the women here."

JENNAE VALE

"I have a newfound respect for her," Tina said. "I can't even imagine what that would be like."

Tina helped Sara get settled in a chair near the fire. Despite the sunny sky, the weather was cooler than she was used to.

"Logan says we're expecting some rain," Sara said.

"Really? It was so sunny outside."

"He's always right. He could be a weatherman in our time," Sara said. "Can you imagine that? He'd be the hottie on the evening news." She couldn't contain her laughter and Tina joined her.

As they sat and continued their conversation, Tina's mind kept wandering up the stairs and into Donal's room.

~

"She feels quite warm again," Donal said, pressing his lips to Elena's forehead as he'd seen Tina do. "Will ye tell Tina before ye leave?"

"Aye. I'll go now," Doreen said.

Donal dipped a cloth in cool water and swabbed Elena's face and body with it. It seemed as if Tina would never arrive, but then the door opened and she hurried in.

"Her fever's back?" she asked

Elena coughed and Tina's face immediately showed concern. "How long has she been coughing?"

"Since I've been back. Is that bad?"

"I don't know. Could be." Tina examined Elena from head to toe. "She's got a rash. I don't like that."

"When will Dr. Ferguson arrive?" He tried to keep the worry from his voice, but it was a futile effort.

"The only thing I know is that he's on the way."

"Ye said that Ashley can contact the witch. Will she help Elena?"

"Yes. I'm sure she will. Go find Ashley. I'll stay here with Elena."

Donal strode from the room, purpose clear on his face. He didn't have to go far to find Ashley. She was in the passageway leaving her chamber.

"Ashley," Donal said before she began descending the stairs. "Elena's fever is back. She has a cough and a rash. Tina thought we should contact Edna."

Ashley immediately turned back towards her room. "Come with me," she beckoned him.

He followed her into the chamber she shared with Cailin. From a chest in a corner of the room she removed an odd globe which she held up in front of her face.

"Edna," she said. "It's me, Ashley. We need you."

A moment or two passed before a woman's voice came from the globe. "Yes, Ashley. I'm here."

"Is that her?" Donal asked.

"Edna, you know Tina's here," Ashley said.

"Of course I do. I sent her."

"Well, the little girl she's been taking care of is really sick. Her Da, Donal, is here with me and he's asking for your help."

"Hold on for a minute while I try to see what's happening."

Donal wasn't sure how she could see what was happening, but he also wasn't sure how he could hear her voice, so he decided he'd just accept it no matter how odd it seemed. The only thing that mattered was getting Elena some help.

"I see now. Dr. Ferguson is still a few days away. Have Donal bring her to the bridge and I'll send them across. We'll get her to a doctor here."

"It is two days ride to that bridge. There's rain coming and Elena should not be out in it," Donal said.

"You're right, Donal. We can't let her get worse. Is there another bridge nearby?" Edna asked.

Ashley glanced at Donal. "Is there?"

"There is one. Not far from here."

"I've only used my bridge here in Glendaloch and the bridge in San Francisco. I'm nae sure it will work, but we can try. How quickly can ye be there?"

"'Tis getting late, but I believe we can be there before the sun sets."

"Go then. I'll watch for ye."

"Thank ye, Edna, and thank ye, Ashley."

Donal pushed all the panic away and focused on what he needed to do as he hurried back to his room. If he thought too much about Elena or traveling through time he would not be able to move. Years of training to stay calm in battle were serving him well. "I'm taking Elena to a nearby bridge. Edna will send for us to come to her." He hurried to wrap Elena in a plaid.

"What about me?" Tina asked.

Donal continued getting ready and didn't answer. He wanted her to join them, but he knew she didn't want to be with him.

"Donal," she touched his arm and he felt her comforting touch bring him a small amount of peace. "I'm coming with you," Tina said.

He nodded, "Hurry then."

Tina ran back to her room and grabbed what little she had in the way of possessions before joining Donal in the hall. They hurried down the stairs and out into the courtyard where Donal's horse awaited them.

"Ashley told me ye were hurrying to get to the bridge before nightfall," Cailin said, handing him the reins. Tina held onto Elena as Donal mounted the horse and Cailin helped boost her and the bairn up in front of him.

Donal wrapped an arm around Tina's waist before clucking to the horse. "Thank ye, Cailin!" he called as they rode out through the gates.

"The bridge is over a day's ride away," Tina said.

"Edna will meet us at one that is closer," Donal said.

"Why didn't Edna use that one to send me here?"

"I dinnae know. I dinnae know how any of this works. I just want Elena to be well. 'Tis all I want," he wanted Tina, too. He couldn't tell her that. She still hadn't forgiven him and she might never.

Tina remained silent as she held Elena in her arms. He was struck by how much they appeared to be a family to anyone they might pass on the road. The truth of it was quite different.

Donal's strong arm wrapped around Tina felt good. Better than good. She was secure and unafraid, knowing that he would see them safely from this time to the next and that they would both do whatever was necessary to get Elena the help she would need. She wanted to tell him she forgave him, but the words stuck in her throat. Why was she so difficult? *She* didn't even know the answer to that question, so she remained silent. She recounted all the times in her life she had been thoughtless and unkind to her sister. Selfishly wanting her to give up her career to stay at home with the family instead of following her passion. Tina wasn't perfect and she knew it, but why did she expect everyone else to be? Why did they all have to play by her rules? Maybe it was time for her to rethink that whole thing. She was going home. Once she got back to her own time she wouldn't be returning. She hadn't had a chance to say goodbye to anyone, but she hoped they knew how much she appreciated everything they'd done for her. Things may not have turned out the way she planned, but it had been an adventure of sorts.

As they rode, the sky began to darken and Tina worried it might get too dark for them to see where they were going. "Logan said it might rain," she said.

"We'll make it to the bridge before it does," Donal said.

"Will we get there before dark?"

"I'm hopeful we will."

"When I get back to my own time, I won't be coming back here with you." There she'd said it.

"I understand."

Tina wasn't sure what she expected him to say or even what she hoped he would say. "Don't worry. Elena will be okay. The doctors there will know exactly what to do."

"I ken ye dinnae wish to hear this, but I'm verra sorry for lying to ye."

"I know you are." Could she say it? Could she tell him what he needed to hear. "Donal…"

"Aye."

"You'll never know how hard it is for me to say this, but I forgive you. I'm learning that no one's perfect, especially not me and I should have given you a chance to explain yourself."

He pulled her tighter against his strong chest where she felt warm and safe. "Thank ye, lass. I didnae want ye to hate me, especially now that yer going back to yer own time and I'll nae see ye again."

"I don't hate you," she protested. Had she really given him that impression.

"My wish is for ye to remember me with some fondness, as I will ye." He placed a small kiss against her temple then sat up straight. The movement put a small amount of distance between them and yet it felt like a chasm.

This was bad. He was tugging on her heartstrings. The sincerity in his voice told her she'd been a fool where he was concerned. Damn her high expectations. But this was what she did. She held every man she met to some unattainable moral code in order to sabotage her own happiness. But why? If she only knew the answer to that question it might solve all her problems. She still had feelings for Donal, but it seemed she was willing to throw that all away because of her own stupid pride.

"Donal, when we get to my time and once we know Elena will be alright, we need to talk. I haven't exactly been fair to you."

"The bridge is just up ahead," he said. "I don't know what we're to do when we get there."

"I think we just wait."

"Maggie," Edna yelled from her office desk. "I need ye."

"Coming," Maggie answered.

A few moments later she appeared. "What do ye need?"

"We've got to get Tina, Donal and wee Elena back here."

"You've done that a million times. Why do ye need my help?"

"This time they're coming from a different bridge. Ye ken I've only worked with the two."

"Oh!" Maggie seemed at a loss. "Can we do that?"

"I don't know, but I hope so. The bairn is quite sick. She needs some twenty-first century medical attention."

"That goodness Dr. Ferguson's nephew took over his practice. What's wrong with her?"

"I'm nae a doctor, lass. Ye ken it."

"Sorry. Silly question."

They stared into the flames of Edna's hearth waiting for the trio to appear.

"I can see the bridge," Maggie said. "Is anyone waiting for them here at our bridge?"

"Yes. I sent Teddy. He should be there by now."

"Well, at least we've got that part covered."

"There they are," Edna said, pointing into the fire.

"What do ye want me to do?" Maggie asked.

"Stay right here with me. I may need some added energy to create the fog."

"Donal, can ye hear me?" Edna asked.

"Aye. Where are ye?"

"Ye cannae see me, but in a moment or two, if all goes to plan, ye'll be surrounded by a swirling fog. Dinnae panic. Can ye keep yer horse calm?"

"Aye. He's as steady as they come," he said.

"Good. Hold tight to each other and before ye ken it ye'll be here. Stay right where ye are now."

Edna closed her eyes, focusing on the fog and the bridge. She repeated an incantation over and over again until she heard Maggie's voice.

"It's working, Aunt."

She opened her eyes just in time to see the swirling fog encircle them and then they were gone.

Donal's arm tightened around Tina's waist as the fog cleared and he saw that they were on a different bridge. The one he knew to be more than a day's ride away. Everything seemed a bit different to his eyes and as he glanced around they came to rest on a man standing there. He seemed to be waiting for them.

"Are you here for us?" Tina asked.

"I be Teddy," he said. "Follow me."

Donal prodded his horse forward. It was fully dark now, but there were balls of light on posts above their heads as they rode, lighting their way. They followed Teddy as he led them to a road with unfamiliar buildings.

"The inn's over there," he said. "I'll take yer horse when we get there."

Donal's body tensed as he glanced around at the strange buildings and other oddities.

"Don't worry. I'm here with you. It'll be alright," Tina said.

"I'm nae worried," he protested. He didn't wish Tina to think him afraid of the things he was seeing.

They arrived at the inn and he dismounted before taking Elena from Tina's arms. It seemed she didn't need his help as she dismounted with ease. "We have horses on our ranch at home," she explained.

Donal handed the reins to Teddy, who walked off down the street as Tina opened the door to the brightly lit inn.

"What candles are these?" he asked, examining a nearby lamp.

"Those aren't candles," Tina said. "They're light bulbs."

"Donal, Tina. Yer here," An older woman with blue hair greeted them and he held Elena a bit tighter. He hadn't known what to expect from a witch, but she had gotten them here and for that he was grateful. "Come in."

"I'm Maggie." A younger woman approached and held out her hand. She didn't have blue hair so perhaps she was not another witch. He took her hand and shook it gently. "Dr. Ferguson will be here soon to see to little Elena."

"I thought Dr. Ferguson was…"

"It's his nephew. Long story, I'll explain it later."

"Come, sit in my office," Edna said.

They passed through the doors and were greeted by a kilted man. "Donal McCabe. I be Angus Campbell."

Donal took in the Highlander, there was something familiar about him. "Angus Campbell? Do I ken ye?"

"Ye may. I'm from yer time and I've been to Breaghacraig. Mayhap ye saw me there. I hope I can help make yer stay here a bit easier. If ye have any questions, I'm the one to ask."

Donal kept his face neutral as he took in his surroundings. He was a Highlander after all. He would never allow anyone to see anything less than a strong, confident warrior. He suspected that Angus might be the only one who knew what he was truly feeling.

"I've got rooms set up for ye upstairs. Tina ye've been here before. Ye'll have the same room. Donal will be right next door. We've put a crib in there but we can move it where ever ye like."

"Thank you, Edna," Tina said.

"So what did ye think of yer adventure?"

"It was amazing," Tina replied, glancing at Donal.

"And now yer the one having an adventure," Edna directed her comment to him.

"Aye. Is this where Hamish is?" He hadn't thought he would ever see his friend again, but perhaps he could come meet Elena.

"He's in California with my sister," Tina answered.

"Where is that?"

"'Tis far from here, lad," Angus said.

"Will I be able to see him before I return?"

"Nae, but ye can speak with him."

How could he speak with him if he wasnae here? They made no sense. Perhaps it was more of the witch's magic.

"Don't worry about it right now. We'll see to it."

A bell rang, "That must be Dr. Ferguson. I'll go see."

Donal could hear voices coming from the entrance as Edna spoke with a man. Their voices got closer before they appeared. "Donal, this is Dr. Ferguson."

"I'm pleased to meet ye, Donal," the man said.

"Can ye help wee Elena?" Donal asked, all the anxiety he'd been feeling bubbling to the surface.

"I believe I can. Let me have a look at her."

"Angus, why don't we go wait in the dining room. Give the doctor more room. Do ye need more light?" Edna asked.

"No. This is fine."

"I cleared my desk and put a blanket there to place her on."

"Perfect."

"We'll be close by if ye need us." She closed the door behind them so it was just the four of them in the room.

"Now, let's see what we can do for the little one," Dr. Ferguson said, taking Elena from Donal's arms and laying her on the cleared desk. He placed a black bag next to her and removed some things Donal was unfamiliar with. Unwrapping the plaid, he put things in his ears and another thing on Elena's chest.

"He's listening to her heartbeat," Tina explained. "And now he's checking her ears."

Donal was fascinated.

The doctor then looked inside her mouth. "It seems she has the measles, the Koplik's spot confirms it," Dr. Ferguson said. "It's good that ye brought her back to this time. The treatment will require plenty of fluids, a fever reducer and time. She should rest as much as possible. We will need to watch for complications. It is rare, but if her fever runs verra high or she develops pneumonia she will need to be hospitalized. What about ye? Have ye both had the measles?"

"I've had the vaccine," Tina said.

Dr. Ferguson looked at Donal, "And ye?"

"I cannae say. I dinnae remember ever having anything like this."

"Don't be surprised if ye get it then. It's highly contagious, but if ye do get it, the same treatment applies." Dr. Ferguson packed his bag and headed for the door. "If ye find she's getting worse or if ye need anything else, I'm just down the road."

"Thank you, Doctor," Tina said.

"Aye. Thank ye," Donal added. It had only taken a few minutes, but Donal felt the weight of the world leave his shoulders.

CHAPTER 13

"I'm going to call my sister," Tina said. "Let her know I haven't fallen off the face of the earth. Do you want to talk to Hamish?"

"How can I do that if he's nae here? Do ye have a magic globe like Lady Ashley?"

Tina's eyebrows shot up at that, "No, it is not a magic globe it's a phone. I will show you."

They went up to their rooms and placed a sleeping Elena down for the night and turned off the light before retreating to Tina's room right next door.

Tina found her phone right where she'd left it. "Oh, good! It's charged."

She could feel Donal standing close behind her. It wouldn't be too hard to lean back into him. Maybe he'd wrap his arms around her, even kiss her neck. Her insides turned to jelly whenever he was near, but she'd pretty much told him to give up and so there was no way he'd make a move. He hadn't touched her unless it was absolutely necessary. And yet, she wanted that touch.

"Now what do we do?" his deep voice rumbled in her ear.

Had he read her thoughts? "I don't know."

"Ye said we could speak with Hamish through this thing."

"Oh! Right, the phone." He meant the phone. She had to talk to Elle. She'd know what to do. She dialed her sister's number and before long Elle's voice came through loud and clear.

"Tina! How's your trip? Have you been having fun?" she asked. And then, "Is everything okay?"

"Yes, everything's fine." How was she going to tell her what happened. "Elle, I didn't tell you before you left but Edna offered to send me back in time."

"What? Are you kidding me? And you went?"

"Is that so hard to believe?"

"Not the part where Edna would send you back, but I can't believe you'd willingly go."

"I did." She was proud of her decision. "I know it seems out of character for me, but I wanted to give it a try."

"Why?"

"I'd like to ken the answer to that question as well," Donal said, tipping his head as he looked at Tina.

"Who's that?" Elle asked.

"Donal, he's come back with me." Tina said, making a face at him.

"Oh my gosh! You and Donal! Hamish!" she yelled. When she came back to the phone, Tina could hear the smile in her voice. "I can't believe it. You went back to find a man."

"Is that what ye did?" Donal asked, the hint of a chuckle in his voice.

"Yes. Edna told me she had someone all picked out for me." Maybe this phone call wasn't such a good idea after all. She gave Donal some side-eye sass.

"And 'twas me?" Donal asked, looking delighted at that news.

"Yes, it was you," Tina begrudgingly admitted.

"What is it?" Hamish's voice came through to them.

"Hamish! Is it really ye?" Donal's excitement caught Tina off-guard, causing her to choke back a giggle.

"Donal!"

"Aye."

"Where are ye?" Hamish asked.

"I'm here with Tina. We're with the witch, Edna. Hamish, I have a daughter." The pride in his voice touched Tina's heart.

"A daughter? Yer a Da?" Hamish asked.

"I am. She's nae well. We had to bring her here." There was silence on the other end of the phone as Tina imagined both Elle and Hamish mulling over that announcement.

"What's wrong with her?" Elle asked.

"Measles," Tina said.

"Oh. Is she going to be alright?"

"Yes. Dr. Ferguson came to see her. She's asleep right now." She snuck a peek at Donal who had a look of wonder on his face.

"I can't believe you planned on time traveling and you didn't say anything to me about it," Elle said.

"I didn't want you to try to stop me," Tina replied. "Don't be mad."

"I'm not. I just thought, you know, since you're my sister that you'd share all your secrets with me."

"And for the last few months we haven't had a single secret between us. Not a one," Tina replied. They laughed at that and Tina felt her body lean into the phone, as though she could get closer to them. She missed her sister, her family. She wanted to go home.

"So, you and Donal." Her sister teased. "When are you coming home? Mom and Dad will be so happy that you found someone."

"Well, it's not quite that cut and dry," Tina said.

"Donal, what did ye do?" Hamish shouted through the phone.

Tina had to laugh as Donal looked like he wanted to run.

"Donal!" Hamish yelled.

"Aye. I'm here. I may have told a lie." He glanced at Tina and then down at his feet.

"You did tell a lie," Tina reminded him.

"Tina stay as far away from him as ye can."

"Hamish, to be fair I'm a Da now. I'm nae the man ye knew before ye left."

"Tina, could ye do me a favor and cuff that idjit on the head to knock some sense into him?"

"Don't worry Hamish, I've got this under control."

"So, Donal isn't coming home with you?" Elle asked. That was a very big question.

"Let's not talk about that now. I was just calling to let you know I'm alright. I'll be staying until Elena is well enough to go back home and then I'll get on the first plane there."

"I'm here if you need to talk," Elle said.

"I know and I might take you up on that. I'll keep you posted."

"Can I talk to Donal for a sec, privately?"

"Sure." Tina clicked off the speaker and handed the phone to Donal who looked unsure of what to do. "Hold it to your ear."

"I'm here," Donal said.

Tina wished she knew what was being said, but the one-sided conversation went on for a while. At some point, Hamish joined the conversation and before Donal handed the phone back to her, he said, "Hamish, I miss ye, my friend. Yer a lucky man."

"Okay, I'll be in touch," Tina said hanging up the phone.

"Tis a wonder!" Donal exclaimed. "Thank ye."

"How was it to speak with your old friend?" Tina asked.

"I am grateful for the gift ye've given me." He never thought he'd speak to Hamish again and though Hamish immediately took on his old role of captain with Donal, he didn't mind it one bit. He'd missed his counsel these past months.

"I'm starving, let's see if we can get some food," Tina said.

They checked in on Elena and she was still sleeping peacefully. So they decided it would be fine to head downstairs to the dining room. They were met at the bottom of the stairs by Maggie.

"I was just coming up to see if ye needed anything," she said.

"Food," Tina said. "I haven't really eaten much lately."

"The food at Breaghacraig didnae suit ye," Maggie observed.

"Not at all. Mary tried to feed me, but a girl can't exist on bread and oats alone."

"Head into the dining room. I'll keep an eye on Elena for ye while ye eat."

"She's sleeping, hopefully she'll be down for a while."

"I'll just hang out in the room so if she wakes up there's someone there." She headed up the stairs.

They picked the table by the fire to sit at. Dylan appeared from the kitchen.

"Hey, you're back," he said.

"Dylan, this is Donal. Dylan is Maggie's husband."

"I remember seeing ye at Breaghacraig. Ye were there when the witch was causing trouble for the MacKenzies."

"So was Maggie," Dylan said. "Although she was in disguise most of the time. I'm guessing you're hungry."

"Yes. We'll take whatever you've got."

Dylan went to the bar and got a bottle of wine and two glasses for them. "You can enjoy this while I get the food together for you." He poured them each a glass and set the bottle on the table.

"Thanks," Tina said.

"I'll be right back."

Donal stood, going to the window and staring out. "What was that?" he asked.

Tina joined him. "Oh, that's a car."

"There were no horses pulling it," he noted. "There's another."

"You'll see lots of those. It's how people get around."

He turned from the window, "I like my horse." He was so focused on what was outside the window he hadn't realized how close Tina was standing. She was even smiling at him. He could reach out and pull her closer, but he knew he shouldn't.

"People still ride horses, but only for fun. Cars are much faster."

He cocked an eyebrow and narrowed his eyes in disbelief.

"It's true!" she said. "Come on let's enjoy the wine."

They sat back at the table, but Donal's attention was diverted by everything that moved out on the sidewalk and in the street.

"This must be unbelievable to you. If Elena is doing better tomorrow we could try to sneak out for an hour. Maybe we can go for a walk and see some of the things you're fascinated by."

"You'd do that? I didnae think ye wished to be with me."

"Donal, I'm trying to get over the lying. I know I'm being too hard on you. It's just that I've been lied to so many times. Old habits die hard in my case."

"Do ye believe I'm sorry?" His eyes pleaded with her for understanding. He didn't know how many times or ways he'd have to apologize, but he'd keep doing it forever if necessary.

"I do. My fear comes from not knowing if you'll do it again."

She was being honest with him and she deserved an honest answer, but he felt it might be better to simply tell her what she needed to hear. "I won't."

"You will. We all do." He couldn't read her. She was looking at him with a certain sadness. He wanted nothing more than to be the man she wanted him to be.

"Even ye?"

"Yes, even me."

"Tina, I want to be yer man. I want a life with ye. That is the truth of what is in me heart." He was bearing his soul to her, but was unsure if he was making any progress.

He could see she wasn't sure how to respond to him. She was afraid. Afraid to give him her heart. "Let's get through dinner first. One step at a time."

"Does it mean yer willing to give me another chance?"

"Dinner first," she said.

~

Dylan brought them plates filled with foods she was familiar with. Chicken, potatoes, gravy and veggies. "Mmmm... You have no idea how good this looks to me."

"The test is whether it tastes as good as it looks," Dylan chuckled as he placed a basket of bread and rolls on the table. "Enjoy."

She dove right into the food, not caring one bit that she was being rude. She glanced up a time or two to find Donal was enjoying the meal as much as she was. When they were done, she wiped her mouth with her napkin and released a satisfied sigh. "No disrespect to Mary, but I missed this so much."

Dylan emerged from the kitchen with a tray of sweets and a coffee pot. He retrieved cups from the bar and poured them each a cup.

"Dylan, the food was amazing," Tina said.

"I'm glad you enjoyed it. What about you, Donal?"

"'Twas the best food I've ever eaten," he replied.

"Wow! That's quite a compliment." He took their empty plates. "Enjoy the dessert and coffee. Stay as long as you like. It's just the two of you tonight."

"I was wondering about that. Where are all your customers?" Tina asked.

"We're officially closed tonight."

"Oh, no! And we made you work."

"I'd be cooking anyway. Edna, Angus and Maggie have to eat."

"I guess they do. Thank you so much for making my first meal back here so wonderful."

As he headed back to the kitchen, he called back over his shoulder, "I'm sure Maggie told you, we're here to help. We'll babysit for you so that you two can have some time together." It sounded like they would definitely get a chance to explore the town a bit.

Tina took a forkful of chocolate cake. "You have to try this," she said to Donal, placing it in front of his mouth. He tipped his head in question. "Go on. I can guarantee you that you've never had anything like it before." He was still examining the fork. "It's sweet."

Donal took it into his mouth and began to chew. His eyes closed in apparent delight.

"It's good, huh?"

"Aye." He took his own fork and loaded it up with more.

"Here, have some ice cream with it." Tina put a spoonful of ice cream in his mouth. This time his eyes flew wide open.

"Mary must know of this."

"She couldn't make it even if she wanted to. She'd need a freezer."

"Will ye show me?"

"Maybe tomorrow."

Tina gazed across the table at him. Her heart fluttered in her chest remembering the brief kisses they'd shared. She hadn't had a chance to discuss her situation with Elle, but deep down she knew exactly what Elle would say. She'd tell her to stop being so stubborn and forgive him already.

"Donal, I don't know what's wrong with me," she said.

"There's nary a thing wrong with ye, lass. Yer perfection," he said, his eyes reflecting her own lustful thoughts.

"We should go upstairs," Tina said,

"Yer right, Maggie will wonder where we've been," he said.

She'd almost forgotten that it wasn't just the two of them. Hope had filled her heart that they might spend the night together, but it wasn't to be. At the top of the stairs they stopped outside of her room.

"Good night," Donal said, caressing her cheek, his eyes traveling over her face.

"Good night. I'm so happy we got Elena here and that she's going to be fine. I'm also happy to share this experience with you." Was he going to kiss her or not?

Donal removed his hand. "I'll see ye in the morn." He opened her door for her and then headed for his own room.

She closed the door behind her. "Damn. No kiss." She thought her signals had been pretty clear, but still he held back. She knew he wanted her as much as she wanted him. Finding time to be alone with him was going to be tricky. They had Elena to think about and everyone else at the inn. She climbed into bed feeling frustrated with the way the night ended.

∼

Donal wasn't sure what to do about Tina. He wanted her and he thought she felt the same, but he was afraid to give her his heart once again only to have his hopes dashed. His main focus had to remain his daughter.

"You're back," Maggie said.

"How is she?" he asked.

"She's better than she was when we first saw her. She actually woke up and we played a bit. That only lasted a little while. Her energy level is a little low, but that's to be expected." Maggie headed for the door. "How was dinner?"

"I've never had anything like it. 'Twas verra good," he replied. "Yer husband is a most talented man."

"And I'm a verra lucky woman. Did things go well with Tina?"

"I'm nae sure. I'm confused by her." Maybe Maggie could help him. She'd been willing to help with Elena and he could see she was a kind lass. His gut told him she would understand.

"How so?" she asked, tipping her head and giving him her full attention.

"I thought she wanted to be my woman, but then something happened and she told me it couldn't be." He shifted uncomfortably and dipped his head ashamed of his behavior.

"What happened?" She encouraged him to continue.

"I led her to believe that I had been married to Elena's mother. It gained me much sympathy, which I needed at the time." He glanced up, expecting to see Maggie's disapproval, but instead he saw a woman who was interested in understanding exactly what had happened.

"I see. Ye would have told her eventually right?"

"I think I would have, but I never got the chance. She said that she forgives me, but there is still something holding her back. I dinnae think she will get past it. I've fallen in love with her. I didnae ever expect to be in love." He went to the crib and placed a hand on Elena's head. He smiled down at her. "I never thought I'd be a Da and now that I am I can't imagine my life without my daughter."

"You're a good man, Donal. If ye weren't, Edna never would have sent Tina back for ye." Maggie's soft, reassuring voice was like a soothing balm to his wounded heart, but no matter how soothing it was, it didn't change the fact that Tina no longer wanted to be with him.

"I wish things were different, but Tina will stay here and Elena and I will return to Breaghacraig."

"It doesn't have to be that way," Maggie assured him. "Edna knows ye were meant to be together. She's not about to give up."

"She'll help me?"

"She will. I'll talk to her. She already knows what's happened, but we'll do whatever we can so that ye and Tina can have some alone time, without Elena. We'll take care of her so ye can work things out with Tina."

Donal took a moment to think about what Maggie was saying. They would help him get Tina back and then he could return home with her and his daughter. It was exactly what he'd hoped for. When he looked at Maggie again, it was with eyes full of hope and a happy grin.

"If things work out the way I know they will, ye'll be able to stay here in this time with Tina and Elena."

This stopped Donal in his tracks. He never said he wanted to stay here. It was an exciting adventure, but there were so many things he didn't know or understand. He'd be completely out of his element. He preferred living where he knew his position and worth.

"I can see from the look on yer face that this is all a little scary for ye," Maggie said.

"I fear nothing," Donal said, puffing out his chest and raising his chin.

"Well, that'll make staying here a lot easier for ye. Tina lives on the other side of the world, as does her sister and Hamish."

Donal was excited at the prospect of seeing his old friend once again, but he remembered that Tina said they lived near her family. He didn't know those people. The Mackenzies had been his only family for a long time. He had visited other clans but always felt lucky he had a good home to return to. "Will they welcome me... and Elena?"

"Hamish is pretty happy there. I think they'll love ye both. I'll see ye in the morning," Maggie said, closing the door behind her.

Donal didn't know what to think. He knew he wanted Tina back but there was precious little else he was sure of. He stood a long time staring down at Elena, watching her chest rise and fall and thanking his lucky stars he had her in his life.

CHAPTER 14

"Good morning!" Edna entered the dining room with an arm filled with books and papers. She stopped beside Tina and scanned the room. "Where's Donal?"

"He's still upstairs. Maggie's showing him how to use a disposable diaper. Things are a lot different here, but he wants to learn."

"Are ye happy with the match I've made for ye?"

"It's been a bit more complicated than I thought it would be."

"We're complicated humans. Something, or in this case, someone worth having is worth working for, aye."

"I think I may have complicated this whole thing more than it's possible to fix."

"How so?"

"Donal lied to me. I've been lied to so many times by guys I was dating that I finally made it something I simply wouldn't tolerate. It's always been a deal breaker for me."

"I see. So his lie is unforgivable. The moment ye found out he'd lied ye lost all feeling for him then because ye think him a terrible person. 'Tis a shame."

"He's not a terrible person. I can see his good qualities. He's a good father to Elena even though it was sprung on him in the worst possible way. He's accepted the responsibility of caring for her. I'm proud of him. I know how tough it's been."

"Have ye told him that?" Edna tipped her head, raising an eyebrow.

"No. I'm afraid I haven't." Tina thought back over their conversations the last couple of days. She had done most of the talking and none of it was kind. In her attempts to convince herself that this match would never work, she had been harsh and judgmental about his past, then dismissed his apologies for telling a lie when he was desperate. What kind of a person was she? No wonder Donal kept his distance last night. "I've let my pride get in the way and now I don't know what to do. What if he thinks I'm not worth fighting for now?"

"So yer going to make him fight are ye? Hmmm… I would think ye might start by letting him know that ye have a foolish idea that the man yer with should be perfect. That he cannae ever make a mistake or you'll be done with him." Edna set the papers down on a nearby table.

"That's not what I said," Tina protested.

"Perhaps not, but maybe 'tis what Donal now believes to be true. Donal is a warrior. He will fight for what he wants, what he believes in. But warriors are also smart enough to take all the factors into consideration so they can protect themselves. If they know they can't win, then there's nae reason to fight. He may believe that at some point in the future he'll do something to displease ye and ye'll reject him all over again. And if 'tis what he believes, then why would he fight?"

"Edna are you angry with me?" Tina got the impression that somehow she'd said or done something that was irritating to Edna.

"I'm nae angry with ye," Edna said and then seemed to rethink it before speaking again. "Well, perhaps a tad. Ye told me ye wanted my help to find the man of yer dreams. I did that, but yer letting yer silly rules prevent ye from finding out what a truly wonderful life the two of ye… the three of ye could have." She threw her arms in the air out of frustration. "Ye act like love is something that just happens, that ye dinnae have to work for it."

Tina thought about what Edna was saying. She wanted to tell Edna she was wrong, that she understood love took work. But she knew that wasn't the truth. Edna was one hundred and fifty percent right. She was the one not doing enough. If she wanted this relationship to work, she was going to have to fight for it. She needed to convince Donal that she wanted him by her side. But after so much time pushing him away, she had no idea what to do.

"Edna please... help me," even to her own ears she sounded desperate.

"Are ye sure? I dinnae wish to put Donal through any more torture than he's already been through."

"I'm sure." She felt the conviction down to her toes. This is what she wanted, she could be a warrior, too.

"Good. Maggie and I will take care of little Elena today. The two of ye will be spending the day together. Dylan is packing ye some food. For now, sit here and have some breakfast."

Tina watched Edna hurry from the room. It seemed she already had a plan. Edna knew before Tina did what the outcome would be. Tina thought about what it would be like to be truly alone with Donal and a slow smile spread across her lips.

∼

Donal opened the door so that Maggie could leave and was surprised to find Angus standing there.

"Good day to ye, lad," he said.

"Good day, Angus."

"Can we talk?"

"Aye. Come in."

Maggie waved goodbye as she left them.

"How's yer wee lassie?"

"She's better today."

"Good. We're going to babysit today so that ye can spend some time with Tina."

Donal was quite surprised. First that they were willing to watch

Elena all day and second that he'd be spending the day with Tina. "I dinnae ken what to say."

"Nae need to say anything, lad."

"And she wishes to spend the day with me?" Donal was a bit skeptical. They were getting along better, but he still wasn't sure what she expected of him.

"She does, but 'twill be yer job to woo her. We cannae do that for ye," Angus chuckled.

Donal sat on the edge of the bed. He looked up at Angus who stood there, hands on hips and looking like the toughest of Highlanders. "How did ye get here, Angus?"

"Edna. I was her first time traveler," he explained, a happy twinkle in his eye. "I knew from the first moment I saw her emerge from the fog that she was going to be mine. It was love at first sight for me and I can say with some certainty that she felt the same.

"Have ye ever made her so angry that she didnae wish to see ye again?" Donal asked.

"Nae. I cannae say that I have. She gets angry with me, but we always talk things through. 'Tis what ye must do with Tina. She's a stubborn one from what Edna tells me, but worth the effort."

"I believe yer right." He'd known it all along he supposed. From the first moment he saw her, something told him Tina was a woman worth knowing.

"Edna has arranged for ye to have the day to yerselves. Ye should go downstairs and have some breakfast. I'll stay here with the little one until Maggie comes for her, but before ye go, I'll show ye one of the modern conveniences ye'll love."

"What would that be?" Donal wondered. Everything he'd seen so far had left him speechless.

Angus led him into the space they called the bathroom. "This is the shower. Now if ye'd rather, ye can bathe in the tub, but the shower is an experience nae to be missed." Angus showed him how it worked, gave him soap and towels and then left him.

Donal couldn't believe how kind these people were. They didn't know him and yet they had opened their home to him and his daughter and now they were going to help him get his woman.

After the most amazing bathing experience of his life, Donal made his way to the dining room to find Tina breaking her fast. "Good morn," he said, he sat across from her feeling quite a bit more sure of himself than he'd been in days.

"Hi. How did you sleep?" she asked.

"Verra well. The bed was even more comfortable than the big bed at Breaghacraig."

"Everything's more comfortable here," she laughed and the sound gave him hope. "Ye could be right. I havenae seen everything yet, so I cannae say. Angus showed me the shower this morning."

"I'll bet you loved that."

"I did."

"I thought you looked all clean and shiny," she teased.

He ran a hand through his wet hair. "Angus tells me that they'll care for Elena today."

"Yes. It's so nice of them." Tina said, glancing at him with appreciative eyes.

This shower must have magical powers. "We havenae spent much time together, just ye and me."

"I guess we really haven't," she agreed.

"I'm happy to spend the day with ye." He wanted her to know that despite the fact Edna had arranged their day together, he wasn't protesting.

She smiled the sweetest smile. One that melted his heart.

Dylan arrived with some breakfast for Donal and a basket of food for their day. "Here you go. Edna's going to tell you what she's got in store for you. She'll be back soon. I hope you like the breakfast, Donal."

He looked at the plate filled with things he wasn't familiar with.

"Those are Belgian waffles, strawberries and whipped cream. There's even some maple syrup. It looks delicious," Tina said.

The aroma wafting up to Donal's nose was all it took for him to know he would love it.

"I wonder what's in the basket," Tina said.

"Don't look now," Edna said, entering the room. "Let it be a surprise."

"Alright. Where are we going?"

"Finish yer breakfast and meet me out in front of the inn. I'll explain it all to ye then."

Tina and Donal exchanged interested glances.

"Curiosity's got the best of me," Tina said.

"I'd have to agree," Donal said. "Do ye wish to go now?"

"No. Finish your breakfast."

He did just that and enjoyed every bit of it. When he was done he quickly finished his orange juice and then wiped his mouth. Standing, he put a hand out to Tina, who thankfully took it. His hopes for this day were great, but somehow he knew that with Edna on his side everything would work out for them both.

"I'm a little nervous," Tina said as they headed for the door.

He took her hand in both of his. "I'm here with ye. I'll take care of ye. Dinnae fear."

She took a deep breath and released it. "Okay. I won't."

"There ye are," Edna said. "Donal, here's a map. I've marked the spot where yer to go. Tina we put the destination into yer phone."

Tina patted herself down searching for something.

"I've got it here, dear. Don't worry. We didn't touch anything else." Edna handed the phone to Tina. "The two of ye will navigate yer way to the spot we've chosen. I think ye'll be quite pleased when ye arrive. There's nae hurry to return. Elena will be fine here with us, so I dinnae want ye to worry about her. Have ye got on good shoes for hiking?"

Tina looked down at her feet. Donal was fascinated with her clothes. Her trewes were tight and showed off every curve. He hadn't been able to fully appreciate her figure while she was at Breaghacraig. He wondered how the men of this time every got anything done.

Angus joined them and seeing the look on Donal's face, laughed. "Ye'll get used to it."

How could Angus say that? Donal hoped he'd never get used to it.

He, too, was now wearing modern clothing thanks to Angus who'd outfitted him with what he called jeans, a t-shirt, and hiking boots.

"Do ye like the new Donal?" Angus asked.

"I do, but I did like the kilt," Tina answered.

"Dinnae fear, we've sent it out to be cleaned and it'll be back in no time."

"Maggie and Dylan are going to go to the shops today. They'll pick up some new clothes for Elena."

Donal had never seen such kindness. The Mackenzies were kind people, but Edna and Angus surpassed even them.

"Off with ye then," Edna said, pointing down the street.

Donal looked at the hand drawn map. It was much like the ones he'd seen at Breaghacraig. Tina's eyes were on her phone.

"I guess we're supposed to compare notes," Tina said, glancing up at him.

They began walking away from The Thistle and Hive towards the outskirts of town. Instead of following the path they'd taken when they arrived, they went further down the road until they reached a spot where they both felt they should head onto a narrow path surrounded by trees and shrubs. All morning long they worked together, stopping occasionally to double check the two maps they were using. Surprisingly they were both very accurate. They'd taken every turn exactly where the maps said they should and now found themselves in an open field.

"We're almost there," Tina said, showing Donal her phone.

He looked at his map. "I believe yer right."

They crossed the field until they came to a small one room cabin nestled beside a small rill and surrounded by trees and bushes that looked as though they'd always been there, framing the cabin as they might if it were in a painting.

Donal set the basket down and looked at the cabin. "It seems there's a note on the door."

Tina removed the paper and read it. "We're to stay here tonight, if we wish." She opened the door, entering the cabin with Donal right behind her. "It's so romantic," she said.

The small room was festooned with garlands of flowers and candles set atop the mantle of the hearth. The windows wore gauzy white curtains and the old wood floors were covered with beautiful rugs that added an extra layer of warmth to the place. Set back against the wall was a bed covered with layers of beautiful quilts and pillows.

Donal couldn't believe his eyes. In all his years of wooing women, he'd never been anywhere quite so perfect. This would be exactly what he'd want for Tina. A place so worthy of the woman he wished to be his, now and forever. A place where he hoped to change her mind about him. He silently thanked Edna. She had handed him a gift he'd never be able to repay her for. He had no idea why she'd chosen him for her matchmaking mischief, but he was grateful.

"We don't have to stay if you don't want to," she said, sounding unsure of herself to his ears.

"I do wish to stay. More than anything."

"Really?"

"Tina, my feelings for ye havenae changed, even though I fear yers have."

"I think the reason Edna sent us here was so that we could figure it all out." She glanced around the room and then turned to him. "Let's go sit out by the water. It's so pretty out there. We should take advantage of it before it gets dark."

Donal picked up the basket he'd left by the door and brought it with them. There was a plaid tucked inside, which he laid out for them to sit on. The sound of the water flowing across the rocks and downstream was soothing to them both. Tina leaned back on her arms and raised her face to the sky. He couldn't take his eyes off of her. She was so beautiful to him and he wanted her to know that. He hoped by the time they left here she would.

Searching the contents of the basket, he found bottles of wine, bread, cheese and fruit along with some other things. All-in-all there was enough food there to last them until the morning. He thought it might be nice to catch a fish for their meal, but first he wanted to enjoy the peaceful sounds of the water, the birds and the soft breeze rustling through the trees.

"This is so nice," Tina said, laying on her back and gazing up at the sky. "I think this might be the first time I've done this since I was a little girl. I remember examining the clouds with Elle. We'd take turns pointing out what we thought we were seeing. Like that," she pointed to a large fluffy white cloud, "it looks like an angel. Do you see it?"

He squinted his eyes, following the path of her finger and was surprised that he did see it. "Aye. There 'tis." Donal removed the heavy hiking boots Angus had given him and stretched out on his side, propped on his elbow. He was enjoying this time alone with Tina. Since he'd first met her, his life had been a whirlwind. They'd had very little time to themselves. Understandably, Elena needed them and so that had been his main priority. Even when she'd kissed him by the well, they'd been surrounded by the people of Breaghacraig going about their business. Thinking about that kiss wasn't in his best interest at this point, so he did his best to put it out of his head. He needed to use his words if he was going to woo her.

"Tell me about yer life here in this time," Donal said. "I know nothing of it."

"You know Elle is my sister," she said.

"I do and I know Hamish is with her, but I want to know about ye."

"There's not much to tell. I live in California with my mother and father. We've got a ranch with cows, horses and other animals. I've got two brothers. One of them is married and has two kids. I'm Elle's tour manager when they're on the road, but they'll be home now for a while so I guess I'm going to have to find something else to do."

He wrinkled his brow, "What is a tour manager?" he asked, wondering why she now must find something else to do.

"It's kind of complicated. You probably wouldn't understand."

"Try. I'm nae stupid."

"I didn't mean that. It's just that there's nothing like it in your time."

"I want to know."

"Alright. Well, I book all the venues for the band, and the hotels. I make plane reservations. I make sure the tour bus is equipped with everything they need. Essentially, I make sure that all they have to do is get up on stage and entertain the crowds that come to see them."

"It sounds like a verra important job."

"I guess it is. So going on tour with them seemed like a good idea, but it wasn't something I ever thought about doing. I'm kind of a homebody. I never like to be too far from my family."

"And yet here ye are."

"I know. Totally out of character for me." She turned her head to look at him. She seemed to be examining every inch of his face, before she looked up at the sky once again. "All I ever really wanted was to live a quiet life in my home town, near my family. I wanted a husband and children and to be able to do all the things that I love."

"Tell me about them," he said, enjoying the sound of her voice and the fact that she was confiding in him for the first time.

"It's kind of boring, really," she said, raising her hands up in front of her face and examining her fingers.

"I'm nae bored, lass. Tell me."

"I like to cook, although the only time that happens is when my mother isn't around. I'd probably be better at it if I got more practice. I like to make things and I've always dreamed of having my own little shop. That's what I really want to do. And that's all there is to tell," she finished.

"There's more to ye than that, lass," he said.

"Not really. I'm a pretty simple person. I don't have any great dreams to speak of. I've been pretty happy with my life, except for my love life."

"Love life. Ye mean ye havenae had a man in yer life"?

"Right. I've been burned more than a few times and so now I guess I'm extra cautious."

Some of the words she used made no sense to him. "Did these men actually burn ye? Do ye have scars?"

She laughed. "No. No. When I say burned, I mean they weren't very nice to me."

He understood what she meant. She'd been hurt by men in the past and he guessed that he wasn't much better. "I'm sorry to hear it. Ye deserve to be loved and treasured."

"What about you? Tell me something I don't know."

"Most people think I'm only out to have fun. They dinnae believe me to be serious or responsible, as I'm sure ye learned from yer time at Breaghacraig."

"I did hear that a few times," she confirmed.

"Ye see, I'm from a family of nine children. I fell square in the middle. Ma and Da worked hard to feed us. They had little time to spend caring for us and so we had to rely on each other. I spent much time on my own, never having to answer to anyone. I found my share of mischief and I found that I liked it. As I got older, that mischief became focused on the lassies. They thought me handsome and I had a way of convincing them to do things they might not otherwise do. I never thought of the consequences of my actions, but I should have."

"How did you end up at Breaghacraig?" she asked.

"My family drifted apart after our mother and father died. I was grown and ready to strike out on my own when they passed. I don't know where my siblings went or where they are now, I've never heard from a one. I rode into Breaghacraig one day thinking I was pretty important. They invited me to take part in their morning practice. I thought I was much better with a sword than I truly was and I found out the truth of it that day when I ended up on my arse more times than I could count. I guess they felt sorry for me, because they asked me to stay on with them. They taught me to be a warrior and they accepted me into the clan. They replaced my family and now I find I have the beginnings of a family of me own."

"Elena," Tina said.

"My wee daughter. I never knew it was possible to love someone as much as I love her and so quickly." It had truly taken him by surprise. "Now that I know that kind of love, I want more of it. I want to share it with someone." His eyes met hers. He hoped they told Tina that it was she he wanted to share it with.

She looked away from him towards the flowing stream. He hoped he hadn't said too much. This was all new to him and he wasn't sure how to proceed. One thing he was sure of was that he could only do so much. It was going to be up to her to decide whether or not she wanted to be his woman and whether she wanted him to be her man. There was a tiny flicker of hope in his heart. He was hoping that by the end of this day it would become a blazing fire.

CHAPTER 15

"Have ye nae fished before?" Donal asked as he plodded into the stream up to his knees.

"Not like this," she answered. Tina wasn't sure exactly how he intended to catch a fish, but one thing she was sure of was that she'd enjoy watching him try.

He stood with his legs set far apart and his hands perched just above the water. His patience was amazing as he stood completely still and waited. He explained that he planned to catch a fish as it swam through his legs.

This was better than anything else she could be doing right now. Donal was so focused on the water that he was unaware of anything else. Especially the fact that she was watching him so closely. Several minutes passed with no success, but he still didn't move. Tina decided she really didn't care if they had fish for dinner and so she rolled up the legs of her pants and silently crept into the water. When she was close enough, she used both hands to splash water at Donal. Much to her surprise, he must have known what she was up to because he lunged for her, grabbing her around the waist. Her feet went out from beneath her and they both tumbled into the water.

Tina shrieked, "It's freezing!"

Donal picked her up, carried her out of the water and lay her on the plaid, he propped himself up over her. "Ye are a wee devil," he chuckled.

"I didn't want to share you with the fish," she explained, "and I wasn't sure how much longer you were willing to stand there."

"Ah, so ye wished to have me attention." He used the edge of the plaid to wipe away a rivulet of water that was trailing from her hair to her face.

Out of breath and incredibly turned on by this man, Tina nodded her head. "I did." She held her breath as his finger traced her lips. She closed her eyes as her lips parted, begging for his kiss.

"Do ye wish me to kiss ye?" His seductive growl was almost her undoing.

"Yes," was her breathless answer.

She waited, eyes closed, to feel his lips on hers, but instead he asked, "How much do ye wish it?" He'd lowered his head so that he whispered into her ear.

"Please, just kiss me," she insisted.

Donal's deep chuckle reverberated through her as his lips met hers, his tongue found an opening and plundered her mouth. Their tongues continued to tangle as Donal moved closer, helped by Tina pulling him down on top of her. She lifted her hips as one leg wrapped around his back.

The fact that they were both soaking wet from their romp in the stream didn't make any difference to her. She snaked a hand under his t-shirt and relished the feel of taut muscle beneath her fingers. She began to undo the button on his jeans, feeling the hardness of him ready to burst forth. She wanted him and she didn't care about anything else. She'd made her decision and now she wanted to seal their union here on the banks of this stream.

Rain began to plop on the ground around them. Tina wasn't surprised that they hadn't noticed the dark clouds rolling in. Why would they? They'd both been completely engrossed in the pleasure of this moment.

"We should get inside," Donal said as he grabbed the plaid and basket.

They hurried inside just as a loud clap of thunder reverberated overhead followed by a bolt of lightning that lit the dark sky.

Tina was shivering partly from the chill of the rain on her skin and partly from the sensual thoughts running through her head.

Donal got a fire started in the hearth before turning back to Tina. "You're chilled," he said, pulling her into his arms and rubbing her back, which sent waves of heat through her entire body. She melted into him. He seemed to notice because his hands stopped rubbing and simply held her close, his chin resting on her head. Tina could hear his ragged breathing matching her own. They stood perfectly still, each afraid to move, afraid to break the spell that had been woven by the sudden rainstorm.

"Donal." Tina's soft voice implored him to look at her.

He moved ever so slightly back, still holding onto her. He tipped his head, his eyes searching hers. He slowly dipped his head so that his lips were near hers, not touching her, but asking her if she wanted more. No words were spoken. This silent question passed between them and when Tina closed her eyes and nodded, Donal's lips tenderly kissed hers. One soft kiss, followed by another, followed by another. Tina responded, still shivering, but this time the rain had nothing to do with it. It was pure adrenaline running through her veins causing her to quiver at his touch.

Donal tried to speak, but Tina put a finger to his lips. She didn't need to hear his promises. She knew him for who he truly was. He was so much more than she had ever imagined. He didn't need to tell her he cared. There was no need for apologies or for him to speak to her of love. He had said those words, she just had to believe it. She knew her own heart and despite all the time she'd spent trying to distance herself from him, she found she had fallen in love with him. For the first time in her life, Tina was ready to let this moment be all that mattered. There was no thinking of tomorrow, there was only right now, here in this little cabin during a thunderstorm that she would remember forever.

Tina moved away from Donal and began to remove her wet clothes. He didn't venture from the spot where she'd left him. Instead, his eyes followed her every move and when she stood there completely naked, he was in front of her in one long stride, gathering her into his arms and kissing her again. This time with more passion and purpose. His hands caressed her back, sliding down each side of her spine to her buttocks. Their calloused roughness on her skin gave her goosebumps.

"You're so soft." His voice was a rough whisper in her ear, just before he nibbled her earlobe and then kissed her neck. His kisses alone were better than any sex she'd ever had.

Tina gave in to them, relaxing her body and letting him hold her up with strong, sinewy arms. Small satisfied mewls escaped her throat inspiring him to continue down her chest to her breasts, where he stopped and lavished them with attention. She ached for his touch, her skin burning with desire.

"Come," he said, taking her hand and drawing her close to the hearth. "I wish to see ye."

The light from the flames cast a golden glow upon them as Donal removed his own clothes.

Wanting to slow things down and enjoy every moment to the fullest, Tina reached into the basket for a bottle of wine and a glass. She poured some for the both of them.

"There's just the one glass," she said as she held it out for him to take.

"Aye, and there's just one bed." He lifted her into his arms and placed her in the center of it. He took the glass from her then put it to her lips. She took a sip and as he pulled the glass away, some ran down her chin and onto her chest. His tongue followed the trail of the wine and continued on a path further and further down until he came to the vee between her thighs. She quivered as he thoroughly explored her body with both his hands and his mouth.

Her hands tingled as she caught the strands of his hair between her fingers and then let them slip through. She was surprised by the silky, softness of it. He glanced up at her as her tongue darted out to moisten her lips and in an instant his mouth was on hers, strong hands holding her head motionless. Firm lips played across hers, leaving her breathless, but she was elated to drown in his kiss. Pushing her hair out of the way, his lips found the sensitive spot on her neck and she shivered, encouraging him to search for more of those tender places where a mere touch led to involuntary moans of pleasure.

Stopping for a moment, Donal refilled the wine glass. He sipped, his eyes never leaving her face as he watched, teasing her and leaving her wanting more.

"Don't stop, please." Her throaty whisper implored him.

"I'm nae done with ye yet, love." he replied, a wicked smile crossing his lips.

He took the wine that was left in his glass and poured it with deliberateness between her breasts, then ran a finger up between them to catch the rivulets before placing it in her mouth. She sucked the fruity liquid from his finger. He withdrew it to trace her lips once again before assailing her with even more passionate kisses. The hardness of his cock rested between her thighs, filling her with anticipation. She opened her legs for him, but he only teased her opening. Tina reached for him and stroked. His sharp intake of breath filled her with satisfaction, egging her onward. A sensual smile appeared on her lips just before she wrapped them around his shaft, wanting to pleasure him as much as he had her. It was his turn to tangle his hands in her hair, pulling slightly. His breathing quickened as she rose above him, placing herself over his manhood and rocking back and forth. His hands reached for her breasts, pinching and pulling her nipples. As her pace quickened, his hands moved to her hips where he guided her movements. The heat of their love making built inside of her, stoking the fire into all consuming flames of desire. Tina rode him harder and faster, all the while wanting to reach her climax and yet wanting the experience to last forever. It seemed she had no choice. Her walls pulsed and spasmed around him as they both reached the destination they sought.

∽

For the first time ever in his life, Donal was at peace. This moment after they'd made love was somehow even more important to him than the act itself. He cradled Tina's head on his chest and wondered how this had happened. How had he fallen so quickly and so deeply in love with this woman? And for the first time, he wasn't thinking about leaving. He didn't want to walk away and move on to his next conquest. He was exactly where he wished to be now and forever. Tina had fallen asleep, resting atop him and he hadn't moved. He didn't want to disturb her, perhaps afraid that if he moved she might disappear and he'd find that this had all been a wonderful dream. So he stayed where he was until she stirred and looked up at him with love filled eyes. That look made him hard again with wanting her.

"Hi," Tina said before she moved to kiss him.

Soft, sweet kisses and the gentle touch of her hand on his face filled him with a happiness he never knew existed before this night.

"It's still raining," she observed.

The rumble of thunder in the distance and the soft patter of rain on the roof grounded him. This was real. It had happened.

"Are ye cold?" he asked

"A little."

He drew her close and covered her with his body. "Better?"

A small, sweet laugh left her lips. "Mmhmmm."

He lifted her chin with his finger, gazing at her face, searching her eyes.

"Yes," she said to his unasked question.

It was his turn to laugh, a deep chuckle erupting from his throat.

His lips met hers, igniting them both with a pure passion to have one another again.

Donal raised himself up over her, driving into her. An immediate sense of being exactly where he belonged overcame him and he never wanted to leave. Tina's hands reached for him, drawing him close so that their bodies touched from head to toe. The friction of their bodies gliding over each other only added to the ecstasy he was feeling. He carefully watched Tina's face, felt her body tense and relax waiting for release and when she was near, he quickened his pace, calling out her name as he collapsed atop her, both satisfied. Tina smiled up at him. His world was complete. Love seemed to be the key he'd been searching for all these years. It unlocked the man he wanted to be, the man he was with Tina.

~

"I don't want to leave," Tina said, her lips pouting and her nose wrinkling.

"Nor I," Donal answered.

They had gathered their things and it was all Tina could do to keep from throwing herself on top of him and tearing off the clothes he'd just put on. This was all new to her. She'd never felt this way about anyone. She'd be overjoyed to spend the rest of her life in this bed with him, but they had to get back. Elena was waiting for them. Hopefully she'd be well enough to travel and then they could make their plans to go home. She was so excited to have Donal meet her family. He already knew Elle and he'd have a Highlander reunion with Hamish. Her little happily-ever-after fantasy ran through her head like a movie.

Donal must have noticed, "Why do ye smile so?"

"Because I'm happy. Happier than I've ever been."

He beamed back at her, seeming quite proud of himself.

"Yes. It's all your fault. You're the one that has me grinning like a fool."

"Must we go?" he asked, looking back at the bed and then at her wearing a very sexy grin.

"Yes. Come on before I change my mind." Tina grabbed his hand and pulled him through the door behind her.

They got about two steps when she stopped, gazing back at the door he'd just closed. "One more time?" she asked.

She didn't have to ask twice, as Donal swept her up into his arms and carried her back inside.

CHAPTER 16

Bursting through the doors of The Thistle & Hive Inn, Donal and Tina were greeted by a sight that brought great joy to their hearts.

"Da," Elena said. Maggie sat beside her with a blanket strewn across the floor covered with toys of all kinds.

"We got a little carried away," Maggie explained.

"I guess you did," Tina replied, going to Elena and picking her up. "You look wonderful. Are you feeling better?"

"The fever's gone and so is the rash," Maggie reported.

"You're back," Edna said, entering the lobby. "I won't ask how it was. All I need do is look at ye."

"Everything was perfect," Tina said.

"Your wee lass is well and will be ready for travel soon," Edna said.

"That's wonderful! We'll just head upstairs and get our things put away."

They made their way upstairs, placing their things in Tina's room.

"I can't wait to take you home. You're going to love California."

"Tina, I love ye," he said. He stood behind her and wrapped his arms around her, pulling her close. "I wish to be with ye, but I dinnae ken how to fit into this world."

She turned in his arms so she could see his face. "Are you saying you don't want to stay in this time with me?" Fear filled her heart. She thought everything had been settled, but Donal seemed to be having second thoughts.

"I'm saying I'm a warrior. 'Tis what I've done my whole life. 'Tis who I am. I want to take care of Elena and I want to take care of ye, but I dinnae ken how I'm to do that here."

"Don't worry about that. We'll find something for you to do. My father always needs extra ranch hands."

"What would I do?" he asked, gazing into her eyes.

"Take care of the cows and horses. Fix things, you know, stuff like that."

"I took care of the animals when I was a lad, but I left that behind when I came to Breaghacraig. I no longer wish to be that young lad. I'm a grown man. I'm a warrior. Better than most with a sword and dirk. 'Tis what I wish to do. Is there nae need for warriors in this time?"

"Well, yes, there is, but that might be hard for you to do." How could she make him understand? She knew being a warrior was where he got his sense of self worth, but that wasn't something he'd be able to do in Livermore.

"Why? I'm one of the finest warriors at Breaghacraig. On a good day I'm even able to beat Cailin and Cormac." He blew out a breath as he ran his hands through his hair, eyes filled with apprehension and maybe even a little fear. "What does Hamish do?"

"Hamish plays in my sister's band. He works with my father and takes care of the horses."

Donal seemed disappointed by this answer, but straightened his shoulders and stood proud before forcefully saying, "I must be useful."

"You will be. It might take some time for you to get used to the way things work in this time, but you don't need to worry about that now. I can take care of everything."

"I cannae have my wife taking care of me. I am the man. I am the one who is to protect ye and Elena and to provide for ye. What kind of man allows his woman to take care of him?"

Tina was getting frustrated. Nothing she said was getting through to him. They'd had such a wonderful time with each other and she thought everything was worked out between them. It wasn't that she didn't understand his point of view. He was from the sixteenth-century after all, but Hamish managed to give up the crazy notion that the man had to be the breadwinner in the family, why couldn't Donal?

"Let's not talk about it anymore. Maybe Edna can help us figure this out." She moved closer, rubbing his arms with her hands.

Thankfully Donal didn't argue the matter any further, instead he pulled her close, wrapping his arms around her waist. Tina nestled into his chest, breathing in the scent of him as he kissed the top of her head. It would all be okay. It had to be.

"I'm going to take a shower, maybe you'd like to join me." She rubbed her hand down the front of his jeans and got an immediate response. "Come on. Let's just enjoy each other for now. We'll iron out the details later."

She didn't have to ask him twice. He lifted one brow and a wicked smile crossed his lips.

∽

They took advantage of the baby sitting services Edna offered and after their shower, slept the afternoon away.

"We should get dressed and go down for dinner," Tina said.

"Will Dylan be cooking again?" he asked.

"I think he does all the cooking," Tina responded.

He quickly put his pants and shirt on and was at the door before she'd even begun to get dressed.

"I'm hungry," he said.

"I'll bet you are." Tina teased. "I think we both worked up quite an appetite."

That sexy smile she loved appeared on his face as he watched her dressing. She met him at the door with a kiss that almost sent them

JENNAE VALE

both back to the bed, but the sound of his stomach rumbling brought them to their senses.

Entering the dining room, they saw that everyone was seated at the table, including Elena, who sat in a high chair attached to the table.

"Look who's having dinner with us." Tina said, giving Elena a kiss on the cheek.

Donal examined the seat. "'Tis quite a useful thing," he commented.

"You'd be amazed at all the baby stuff available in our time. All to make mom and dad's life easier. And make baby's life safer," Maggie said.

Tina sat on one side of Elena and Donal the other.

Dylan brought the food to the table and everyone helped themselves to the delicious fare he prepared for them.

"So what is yer plan?" Edna asked, passing a bowl of roasted potatoes to Angus.

"Well, we wanted to talk to you about that," Tina said. She took a quick peek at Donal, who was busy looking over the food. "Donal is worried that he won't find his place in our time, because he's been a warrior for so long."

At the sound of his name Donal glanced up from the food, tipping his head in question.

"Is this true?" Angus asked. "Are ye worried about staying in this time?"

"I cannae allow my woman to take care of me. I must be the one who provides and cares for my family." The stubborn set of his chin and the gruff tone of his voice were making it clear to Tina that this wasn't going to be a battle easily won.

"I understand yer concern," Angus said. "I wasnae sure I could live in this time either, but Edna helped me to see that there is more to life than wielding a sword and dirk."

"I dinnae ken what that could be." Donal was dismissing the conversation. Tina couldn't believe it. It was obvious he had no wish to even listen to what they had to say.

"So are ye saying ye don't want to stay in this time?" Maggie asked.

"I wish to return to Breaghacraig."

Tina thought her head might explode. Sure, she knew he was nervous about leaving his world behind, but she thought he loved her and that because he did he'd be willing to take a leap of faith and stay with her. She shook her head and turned to Donal. "And what about me?" she asked.

"You'll come with me. The other ladies like it there, and ye liked them. So ye will be happy there," he said.

Tina couldn't believe her ears. Had he just ignored everything she had said about wanting to live near her family? He thought that just because he said so, she was going to go with him. She clenched her fists in her lap, doing her best to control the panic that was beginning to well up inside of her. She had spent most of her time in the past hungry and wishing she could be home. She had been very clear that she wasn't going back there. "What if I don't want to?" she asked through gritted teeth.

There was silence at the table as everyone waited for Donal's response.

He glanced around at all of them, settling his gaze on Tina. "Then I will go back without ye."

Tina was shocked. She hadn't seen this coming and from the looks of the others at the table, neither had they.

"If you'll excuse me," Tina got up and ran up the stairs to her room. She couldn't breathe. She had finally admitted to herself and to Donal that she loved him and now the unthinkable was happening. She didn't know how to make this right. She wanted to be with him and little Elena, but she wasn't going to live in another century and desert her entire family. She knew it wasn't the same, but it felt an awful lot like being tossed aside. Again. This seemed like a hopeless situation. He wasn't willing to fight for her. She did the only thing she could think to do. She picked up her phone and called her sister.

"Tina, what's wrong? Are you crying?" Elle asked.

Tina managed to pull herself together enough to answer. "Donal

JENNAE VALE

doesn't want to stay in our time. He wants to go back with Elena. I don't know what to do."

"Mom and Dad would be devastated if they never saw you again and so would the rest of us."

Tina couldn't seem to stop crying.

Elle let her cry for a while then gently said, "Come home to us. It'll be alright. I promise. Maybe if you tell him you're leaving he'll change his mind. But no matter what, just make the reservation and get on the plane."

"Alright." She hung up from Elle and immediately made a reservation on the first flight home the next day. Then she locked her door, got into bed and cried herself to sleep.

~

Donal knew he was being unreasonable, but this was a big step for him to take and the fearless warrior was afraid. He was afraid of leaving everything he knew behind and heading into a future full of unknowns. Maybe he wasn't as brave as he thought he was, but if he couldn't at the very least take care of a wife and child then he had no business staying. He hadn't bothered Tina last night. He had a lot to think about and he knew she would be very upset with him. He hoped that when she came down to breakfast this morning she would understand that this was the only way and she would consent to going back with him.

He sat alone in the dining room unable to eat the huge breakfast Dylan set before him. They'd all tried to convince him things would work out if he'd only stay, but he'd put up a wall to the notion that it was alright to let Tina take care of him.

He heard Tina speaking with Edna in the lobby and he got up to see what they were talking about. To his surprise, she stood there with a small, strange looking trunk and he heard Edna say, "I see yer packed and ready to go."

"Where are ye going?" he asked.

"I'm going home," she said. "I won't go back with you and you won't stay here with me, so there's no point in my being here anymore."

He felt as though he'd been stabbed in the heart, but Tina was right. It didn't seem that they were going to come to any agreement here.

Edna glanced back and forth between the two of them. "I dinnae know how to fix this. Ye ken ye belong together."

They both shook their heads in agreement.

"Kiss Elena goodbye for me," she said.

"I'll get her, ye can kiss her yerself," Donal said. Maybe if she saw Elena, there'd be a chance she'd change her mind. He turned to leave them, but Tina halted him before he even took a step.

"No. It would hurt too much."

"Why do ye do this then?" he asked.

"I told you already. I love you Donal and I'll never forget you or Elena, but I won't go back there with you."

A horn honked outside. "That's my ride," Tina said. "Goodbye, Edna. Thanks for a wonderful adventure."

"You're welcome, dear. I'm so sorry things didn't work out."

They followed her out the door, where a car waited. The man driving got out and took her trunk and then Tina got into the car. She looked out the window at them, tears streaming down her cheeks and she waved as the car sped off.

"Ye daft idjit!" Edna said to Donal as they stood together on the sidewalk. "What were ye thinking? She is the perfect lass for ye. And more importantly the perfect mother for Elena. I dinnae know what to say."

Donal knew she was angry with him. He was angry with himself, but it made no sense that he could see for him to stay and not be able to be the man he wanted to be. He stood there heartbroken, watching the car disappear in the distance.

"I'm sorry, Donal. I know ye love her," Edna said, taking him by the arm.

They walked into the inn together and were met by Maggie, holding Elena, Dylan and Angus. They all wore expressions of sadness that only served to make Donal feel worse.

"When can we go back?" he asked Edna.

"I think in a day or two. Dr. Ferguson wanted to see Elena one more time to make sure she was completely well. After that I'll send ye home." The resignation in Edna's voice, echoed his own mood.

Donal took Elena from Maggie and went back upstairs wondering if he'd made the right decision.

"What can we do Auntie?" Maggie asked.

"I'm nae sure," Edna said. Everyone was a little teary eyed after seeing what had just occurred. "There must be something."

"We know Donal just wants to be the provider for his family. How can we make that happen?" It was obvious that Maggie was determined to fix this problem.

"That's the puzzle we must solve. We'll keep him here for as long as we can until we have an answer. We all need to work on this. No idea is too crazy," Edna said.

Angus and Dylan both wore skeptical looks.

"Why do ye look that way?" Maggie asked.

"I don't think you know what a daunting task this is going to be," Dylan said.

"Daunting has never stopped us before and it's not going to stop us now."

"Alright," Dylan said. "If I think of anything I'll let you know."

"Promise," Edna said.

"I promise."

"Angus?" she said, looking to him for support.

"I'll do whatever I can, my sweet. Dinnae fear, we'll find an answer."

But as the days wore on, it was becoming increasingly clear that they weren't going to find an answer and it was getting harder and harder to find excuses for why Donal should stay. Dr. Ferguson didn't care for the idea of lying about little Elena's health. "She's fine. She should be able to go home. I can't keep telling him we need to wait," he said after his last visit.

Edna had just about given up hope, and needed to do something to keep her hands busy. She decided dusting the rooms would be a good distraction and while doing so found exactly what she needed.

"Maggie, I've got it!" she cried, running down the stairs.

"What is it?" Maggie came out of the office to see what Edna was yelling about.

As Edna explained her plan, Maggie's face went from confused to excited. "Ye just might be on to something!"

"Aye. I'm so excited. I think this might be just what we need. Donal has been miserable. He hardly says a word and he has no appetite. Elena is the only thing that keeps him going."

"Let's hope this works then."

∽

"If I ever lay eyes on Donal again, I swear I'll beat him to a pulp," Hamish said as he watched Tina moving her food around on her plate but not eating.

She'd been home over a week now and had done nothing but mope around. Her eyes seemed to be permanently red rimmed from all the crying she'd done and no one in the family seemed to be able to soothe her. She hadn't even unpacked her bags.

"Hamish, I don't think that's helping anything," Elle said.

"What are we to do? I dinnae believe I've ever seen anyone so miserable in all my years."

"That's a bit of an exaggeration, don't you think?" Elle said, rolling her eyes at him. "Tina, let's go unpack your bags."

Tina looked up from the table. She'd heard everything they were saying, but she seemed unable to dig herself out of the black hole she'd fallen into. Maybe Elle was right. The least she could do was unpack. "Alright," she muttered, heading down the hallway to her bedroom.

She opened her suitcase and started tossing clothes on the floor.

"Laundry," she said. She handed Elle her shoes and she put them in the closet. As she neared the bottom of the suitcase, she saw an envelope and remembered that she was supposed to give a note to Zeke, but there was only one envelope and it wasn't the one addressed to him.

"Oh, no! Sara gave me a letter to give to her brother. I feel terrible about it. She was so nice to me and the one thing she asked me to do, I screwed up." She scavenged around in the bottom of the suitcase, hoping to find it, but it wasn't there.

Tina sat on the floor next to her bag and opened the other envelope Sara had given her. Inside she found the recipe for the tea. Ayla's Blend was written at the top in big bold letters. She held it close to her chest.

"What's that?" Elle asked.

"A recipe," she replied.

"For what?"

"Tea. Do you remember Sara? She wanted me to say hi from her," Elle nodded. "When I was at Breaghacraig, Sara made this wonderful tea and I had an idea that maybe I could open a little tea shop here in town."

"That sounds like a great idea," Elle said, taking the note from her hands.

"It is, isn't it?"

If anything was going to get Tina out of this funk, it would be this. She'd throw herself into this new venture and it would help her to forget about Donal, or at least make it so that she could get through a single day without tears.

"Well, let's get to work on it," Elle said. "I haven't got anything to do right now, so it's perfect timing. We'll need to check First Street and see if there are any shops available and then we can go in search of the perfect herbs for the tea."

"What do you think of making it a little book shop, too? You know, maybe used books. People could come in for some tea and scones and they could read books right off the shelf or even buy them."

"Great idea. And you could do a fancy high tea in the afternoons. You know, with little tea sandwiches and petit fours."

Tina was actually starting to feel excited about this. "Yes, I'm doing it."

"I'll call our real estate agent. Maybe she can help locate a shop."

"I'll finish up here," Tina said, as Elle headed off to tell the rest of the family.

CHAPTER 17

They found the perfect spot for the tea shop in a cute little building right in the center of town. There was a vacant shop next door and on the other side was a beautiful antique shop. Tina and her family spent the next few weeks painting and decorating the space. She made parcels of Ayla's blend and stocked the shelves with it. She tried other blends and if she liked them, she ordered what she needed and put them out for sale as well. She worked with her mother on the food. Bobby Carrera was more than happy to be involved. She made scones, muffins and an assortment of other items that would go perfectly with the tea. Small tables were set around the shop and bookshelves were filled with used books they got from friends and neighbors. They would also encourage their customers to leave used books for others to read.

On opening day, Tina was beside herself with excitement. This was what she needed. It would keep her busy now that her job as tour manager was over. Everything about her shop reminded her that she was a strong, resourceful woman and she was doing exactly what she wanted to do.

There was a line of customers waiting for her to open, which only confirmed her decision to open a tea shop downtown.

"This is amazing," Elle said. "I'm so proud of you."

"Me, too," her mother chimed in. "Look what you've done in a few short weeks."

The men of the family all tried to stay out of the way of the customers. Her brothers took turns manning the cash register, while Tina, her mother and Elle visited with all their customers. Hamish stood outside the shop greeting people as they entered. He wore his kilt for this special occasion, knowing that women in this time seemed to love it. And it wasn't just the kilt they loved, they seemed to love him as well.

The local paper showed up and interviewed her for a series of articles they wanted to do on local businesses. Even more exciting was the fact that everyone was happy with their tea and her mother's baked goods. Customers were telling her how happy they were to have a place to go that was dedicated to tea. There were so many coffee shops in town, but because many of them didn't drink coffee, they were overjoyed to have their own special place to enjoy their favorite beverage.

Ayla's Blend was flying off the shelves and received rave reviews from those who tried it. People were intrigued with the fact that it was from an authentic medieval recipe, which was reflected in the packaging. Everything was going perfectly in her life, except that Donal and Elena weren't here with her. The sadness she felt thinking about them was overwhelming, even after all this time. Her first day had been a success, but she was happy that the last customers were leaving so that she didn't have to keep up her cheery appearance.

She locked up the shop and noticed that someone seemed to have rented the empty space next to hers. It would be good to have neighbors on either side of her, she thought as she got in her car to drive home. At some point the pain she felt on losing Donal and Elena would have to diminish, wouldn't it? She wasn't so sure, but for now at least she had something to occupy her mind for several hours every day. It would all be okay, she had to believe that.

What happened when she went home was another story all together. There, alone in her room, she was consumed by her loss. She hadn't quite come to grips yet with the fact that she'd never see them again. She tried everything to forget them. She even tried telling herself that it had all been a dream and they'd never been real, but remembering the feel of Donal's arms around her and the way he had loved her, always brought her back to reality. Her senses betrayed her. If she closed her eyes and thought really hard she could feel his touch, his kiss, his presence. Her nose picked up the scent of pine and leather wafting through the air and she thought of him. There were times when she thought she could hear his low whisper in her ear and she would turn expecting to find him. But he wasn't there and he never would be. She should try harder to forget him, but she didn't want to. He'd always hold a special place in her heart and she was going to have to accept that.

Over the next few weeks, Tina noted the progress next door. They were working hard to complete whatever was going in there. The windows were covered with paper, so she couldn't see in and there was no sign up to give her a clue. She'd have to wait and be patient, two things she was terrible at.

Then one morning, she was out front watering her plants when she heard a familiar voice.

"Tina?"

She didn't look up. No. It couldn't be, but it sounded just like him.

"Tina," he was standing right next to her. "Look at me."

She lifted her eyes to see the man she never thought she'd see again. "Donal! You're here!" She was in his arms before he could say another word.

He held her tight, kissing the top of her head. "Tina, I've missed ye so."

She couldn't speak. Was this real? Was it really him?

Tina found her voice. "How? Why?"

"When ye left, Edna found the note ye were supposed to give to

Zeke. She remembered he ran a medieval martial arts studio in San Francisco and called him."

A tall, handsome man was behind Donal on the sidewalk. He extended his hand to her, "Hi, I'm Zeke Barrett."

"It is so great to meet you! Your sister is the inspiration behind my shop. I'm so sorry. She gave me a letter for you and I lost her letter. I have felt terrible about that for weeks."

"It all worked out. Edna found it and made sure I got it. That letter is the reason I decided to expand. We are opening a Medieval Martial Arts Studio here. I've hired a great guy to run it for me. He's pretty good with a sword and dirk."

Donal gave him a playful shove, "Better than pretty good."

Tina let that sink in, "Are you…? Are you really staying?"

"Aye. I'm working for Zeke now. He has been training me for a while and now this will be mine to run." He wrapped his arms around her and she could feel the clouds lifting, "I'll be able to provide for ye and Elena. 'Tis all I wanted."

"Where is Elena?" she asked.

He grinned, "She's in the studio with Brenna," Donal said.

"I love you, Donal McCabe, but I've got to get my hands on my little girl." She let him go and ran past Zeke into the studio, there she was greeted by a beautiful woman about her age who must be Brenna.

"Elena!" she cried, scooping her up into her arms.

"Mama," Elena said.

"Yes, baby, I'm your mama." Happy tears streamed down her cheeks. She found herself enveloped in Donal's arms as he hugged the two of them.

"We're going to be a family now," Donal said. "If ye'll still have me."

"Of course I will. I've thought about you every day and I was so sad that I would never see you again." She touched his face wanting to be sure he was real. "My family will be so surprised."

"I don't think so," Zeke said. "They've been in on this from the beginning."

"What? Are you kidding me? They're not that good at keeping secrets."

"They did a good job with this one," Zeke chuckled. He and Brenna stood with their arms around each other, smiling the biggest smiles.

"We're so verra happy for ye," Brenna said.

"Thank you," Tina said, "but I'm going to ring a few necks when I get home. I can't believe they didn't tell me."

"We wanted to surprise ye," Donal said before planting a kiss on her lips. "I've missed ye so much."

"I'm going to close the shop," Tina said. "I can't possibly work today."

"Donal, why don't you go home with Tina. We'll finish up here and then we'll be joining the Carreras for the big celebration."

Tina took Donal's hand and walked him next door, where she turned the sign on the door to closed. She pulled down the shades and locked the door.

"This has got to be the happiest day of my life," Tina said.

"I'm so in love with ye," Donal said. "I would have found a way to come to ye even if Edna hadn't arranged all of this. I never want to be parted from ye again."

"Never," Tina agreed.

The celebration at the Carrera's was a big one. Tina was shocked to see that they'd strung lights all around the courtyard, hired a band and that her mother had allowed a caterer to provide all the food.

"Donal!" Hamish nearly crushed Donal in a hug when they arrived. "If ye ever do anything like this again to our Tina, I'll personally beat the tar out of ye."

"'Tis good to see ye, too, Hamish," Donal chuckled. "Now, if ye'll let me go, I need to breathe."

"Sorry. I've missed ye, my friend. 'Twill be good to have ye here with us."

"Hamish and I were talking and we thought you should probably have your own place. It might get a little crowded living with Mom and Dad," Elle said.

"Aye. We've got plenty of room on our property for another house for ye and yer family."

"What? Really?" Tina said.

"Really!" Elle replied.

"It will take us some time to build, so ye'll stay with the Carreras until it's finished," Hamish said.

Tina introduced Donal to the rest of the family. Her father and brothers all gave him almost the exact same warning Hamish had, but then they were patting him on the back and letting him know how welcome he truly was into the Carrera clan.

Zeke and Brenna arrived a little later and joined in on the festivities. Elena met her cousins and they were thrilled to play with her. "Built in baby sitters," Tina said to Donal, who wore a smile from ear to ear.

"When will everyone go home?" he asked.

"Soon. Why?"

"Because I cannae wait to get ye alone, lass. 'Tis been much too long."

Tina's heart and stomach both fluttered at the thought of what was waiting for her later in the night. "I happen to know about a little cabin nearby. Hamish built it when they first moved next door. It's a little more private than my parents house."

"Well, I hope they're willing to let us use it for the foreseeable future," his low, sexy growl sent a rush of heat coursing through her veins.

"I'm a very lucky girl," Tina said, wrapping her arms around her man's neck and kissing him for all she was worth.

EPILOGUE

The end of a long week couldn't have come soon enough Tina thought as she finished her daily routine of cleaning up the tea shop. Tea cups were cleaned and put away, day-old baked goods boxed up for delivery to a local group that fed the hungry, books shelved and dusted. She took one final look around and was pleased that everything was where it should be. She was tired, but feeling a bit giddy as she grabbed her purse from behind the counter. She turned the sign in the window to closed and walked out the front door, locking it behind her. Tina smiled as she saw her handsome Highlander doing the same at the medieval martial arts studio next door.

"Hey, sweetie," she said, as he approached.

Donal took Tina into his arms and kissed her until her knees went weak. It had been six months since he surprised her in this very spot and his kisses always had the same effect. "Are ye ready, love?" he asked.

"Date night has officially begun." Tina gazed up at her man. Oh, how she loved him. "Elena is all set with her cousins for the night. No one is expecting us home any time soon, so it's just you and me, baby."

"I like the sound of that." Donal's hand lingered at her waist as he guided her off down the street.

"I thought we'd have some dinner and then maybe go to that movie you wanted to see." Tina leaned into Donal, loving the feel of him at her side and the warmth his body emitted on this chilly fall evening.

"Where will we go?" he asked, his eyes lovingly locked on hers.

"How about that great little Italian restaurant just down the street? We can walk there and then the movie theater is just a short walk from there." She knew how much he enjoyed Italian food, so she was sure he'd be happy with her choice.

"Ye know me well, lass." Donal's crooked grin always got to her. He had really embraced living in the future. He played video games with her brothers and ran all the studio's social media sites. He loved taking videos of his students showing off their moves and it was exciting to see how well he was doing. At home they had become a real team in parenting Elena, who seemed to have skipped walking and went straight to running after her cousins. Their new home was almost ready for them to move in, but in the meantime, they had been staying in her parents' house. It was busy and loud, but it was full of love. She couldn't believe how lucky she was.

She stopped and faced him. "Donal, have I told you I love you today?"

He looked up, placing a finger on his chin. "I dinnae believe ye have."

"I love you," she said. "I don't want a day to go by without telling you how much you mean to me."

"I love ye, too. I hope ye know it. I hope I've shown ye every day."

"You have." She stood on tiptoe to softly kiss his lips.

Once they got to the end of the block, Tina peeked into a shop window and waved at Mrs. Winston. She stopped moving her flower buckets into the refrigerated case to wave back.

"Wait here a moment, right where I can see ye," Donal said.

"Why?" Tina asked.

"Ye'll see." Donal entered the flower shop where she watched him smiling and laughing with Mrs. Winston. She went into the back and returned with a bouquet of flowers. Donal nodded to her before joining Tina outside. "For ye, my love."

Tina's eyes teared up. It was a bouquet of wild flowers, much like the ones she'd received on their very first date at Breaghacraig.

"Dinnae cry, my sweet. I thought ye'd like them." His thumb brushed a wayward tear from her cheek.

"They're happy tears. I love them." She grasped his hand, holding it up to her cheek. "We had a rocky start, but I know in my heart that you and I were meant to be."

"I'm happy here with ye. Yer a good ma to Elena and I cannae wait to have more children with ye."

"We will," she said, trying not to smile.

His eyebrows shot up in hopeful surprise. "Do ye have something to tell me?"

"Well, I was going to wait until we were at dinner, but yes. We're having a baby!"

Donal lifted her off the ground, twirling her around and around.

"Whoah! Donal!"

"I'm sorry. Did I hurt ye?" He placed a hand on her belly.

"No. Just made me a little dizzy. Maybe we could not do that again."

"Ye have my word." Donal placed an arm around her shoulders and one hand on her elbow as he began escorting her down the street. "Are ye sure yer having our bairn?"

"Yes, of course." When the question in his eyes didn't change, she said, "You know, we've been putting in a lot of hard work and this is your reward." She had to laugh at the comical expression on his face. He was still holding her as if he thought she needed all the help in the world just to walk. She took his face in her hands and looked deep into his eyes, "Donal, I'm okay. You don't have to treat me like I'm going to break," she laughed as she kissed him on the nose.

"I dinnae know what to do."

The poor guy looked like he might pass out. Tina couldn't help but giggle. "You won't have to do it alone, we'll figure it out together. Come on, let's get some dinner. I'm eating for two now."

A NOTE FROM JENNAE

Thank you so much for reading Saved By Time. If you enjoyed the book and have a minute to spare, I would really appreciate a short review on the page or site where you bought the book. Your help in spreading the word is greatly appreciated. Reviews from readers like you make a huge difference in helping new readers find stories similar to Saved By Time.

If you'd like to know when my next book comes out and want to receive occasional updates from me, then you can sign up for my newsletter here http://eepurl.com/bf1CqP

ACKNOWLEDGMENTS

Thank you to Sheri McGathy for the beautiful cover you created for Saved By Time.

Thank you to my editor, Jen Graybeal, for putting the polish on my book.

A very special thank you to Maria Witte for suggesting the name Elena for Donal's sweet wee lass.

ABOUT THE AUTHOR

Jennae Vale is a best selling author of romance with a touch of magic. As a history buff from an early age, Jennae often found herself daydreaming in history class and wondering what it would be like to live in the places and time periods she was learning about. Writing time travel romance has given her an opportunity to take those daydreams and turn them into stories to share with readers everywhere.

Originally from the Boston area, Jennae now lives in the San Francisco Bay area, where some of her characters also reside. When Jennae isn't writing, she enjoys spending time with her family and her pets, and daydreaming, of course.

ALSO BY JENNAE VALE

THE THISTLE & HIVE SERIES
A Bridge Through Time - Book One
A Thistle Beyond Time - Book Two
Separated By Time - Book Three
A Matter of Time - Book Four
A Turn In Time - Book Five
All In Good Time - Book Six
A Long Forgotten Time - Book Seven
Awakened By Time - Book Eight

THE MACKALLS OF DUNNET HEAD
Her Trusted Highlander - Book One
Her Noble Highlander - Book Two
Her Mysterious Highlander - Book Three

A THISTLE & HIVE CHRISTMAS

A HIGHLANDER IN VEGAS

ROSS - THE GHOSTS OF CULLODEN MOOR BOOK 39

Made in the USA
Coppell, TX
30 January 2023